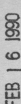

Is Far From Interesting."

Brock stopped suddenly and turned quickly to face her. "I live for today, and I work for the future. Period. End of story."

"Fine!" Jamaica said fiercely, and swept past him.

His stomach rolled over at the hurt look on her face. When he reached out to stop her, she flung his arm aside and kept walking. "Hold on."

"Why? Aren't we in a big hurry to get back to my grandfather's ranch? I know I am. The sooner I can get away from you, the better."

"Jami!" he barked, and she finally stopped. "You don't mean that," he said softly.

She whirled around to face him, and he was surprised at the bitter intensity in her flashing eyes. "Maybe I do! Maybe I want to get away from here before I do something out here I'll regret."

"I'd make sure you wouldn't regret it."

Dear Reader:

Sensual, compelling, emotional . . . these words all
describe Silhouette Desire. If this is your first Desire,
let me extend an invitation for you to sit back, kick
off your shoes and enjoy. If you are a regular reader,
you already know what awaits you—a wonderful
love story!

A Silhouette Desire can encompass many varying
moods and tones. The books can be deeply moving
and dramatic, or charming and lighthearted. But no
matter what, each and every one is a terrific romance
written by and for today's women.

I know you'll love March's *Man of the Month*,
Rule Breaker by Barbara Boswell. I'm very pleased
and excited that Barbara is making her Silhouette
Books debut with this sexy, tantalizing romance.

Naturally, I think *all* the March books are
outstanding. So give into Desire . . . you'll be glad
that you did!

All the best,

Lucia Macro
Senior Editor

JESSICA BARKLEY

MONTANA MAN

SILHOUETTE *Desire*

Published by Silhouette Books New York

America's Publisher of Contemporary Romance

SILHOUETTE BOOKS
300 East 42nd St., New York, N.Y. 10017

ISBN: 0-373-05556-0

First Silhouette Books printing March 1990

Books by Jessica Barkley

Silhouette Special Edition
Into the Sunset #406

Silhouette Desire
Montana Man #556

JESSICA BARKLEY

lives on a small farm in Wisconsin with her husband, their daughter, five horses, fifteen cats and one dog. An avid reader, Jessica also enjoys traveling and distance riding. She has been writing stories since grade school, and although she has published several magazine articles, her true love is romantic fiction.

To Carla for her encouragement;
to Michelle for her silly bets;
and to Jenny, Michael, Rick, Chris and Shaun,
who were all left out last time

One

The party was in full swing when Jamaica McKenzie slipped outside to the solitude of the balcony. Perhaps a billion city lights were lit below her, sparkling like diamonds nestled on black velvet. From somewhere off in the distance came the screaming wail of a police car siren. Above, a commercial jet roared through the sky. And behind her, music from a several-thousand-dollar stereo mixed with a steady buzz of voices to invade her ears. She'd left the room to escape from the noise and commotion. But where after all, in New York City could you ever really find quiet?

At the staccato sound of high heels approaching, she sighed and took another sip of her wine cooler. Why couldn't anyone leave her alone for even a little while, she thought with a touch of irritation.

"Jami, here you are. Are you feeling all right?"

"Sure, Linda," she answered her friend. "I'm feeling just great."

"Now why don't I believe you?" Linda asked softly. "You haven't been yourself all night. Want to talk about it?"

Jami slowly swiveled her glass and pretended to be fascinated watching the pink liquid swirl around the ice cubes. "Not really," she said at last.

"Jami, you're not still thinking about Tracey, are you?"

Jami turned to face Linda and gave her what she hoped was a reassuring smile. "No, I'm not. I'm just a little tired, that's all. Probably too much partying lately. I think I'm going to get my things and head home."

"Already?" Linda protested. "It's not even midnight yet. You're going to offend your hostess."

Jami chuckled. "Well, since you happen to be my hostess, I don't think there's much danger in that. I know you understand."

"I understand a lot more than you realize," Linda replied. "I'll call down to the doorman and have him hail you a cab, if that's what you want."

"Thanks, Linda. I'll talk to you tomorrow." Jami brushed past her friend as she walked into the living room of the expensive penthouse.

A glance around told her the party was just starting to get lively. Several months ago, she would have been right in the middle of it all, having the time of her life. But now . . . now she felt as if she was a stranger here in this roomful of people she had known for years. Lately, she'd begun to look at them in a different light, and she found she had little tolerance for their overindulgences. In fact, the plain and simple truth of it was she felt like an outsider, as if she didn't belong. And more than anything else, she felt restless and bored.

Jami McKenzie bored? The notion surprised even her. All her life, she'd never once thought of herself as being bored. After all, she was the daughter of Jason McKenzie, one of the wealthiest men in New York. She had more money than she could possibly know what to do with. Other than the time she devoted to volunteer work, she was free to do whatever pleased her at the moment. So why in the world should she be bored?

Once she was safe in a cab and on her way to the penthouse she still shared with her parents, she let her mind reflect on Linda's concern. She'd lied to Linda when her friend had asked her if she was thinking about Tracey. Jami had, in fact, been able to think of little else these past few months.

Tracey's tragic death haunted her waking hours as well as her dreams. But the irony was, she'd never really been that close to Tracey. It wasn't that she was mourning the loss of a good friend. Rather, what was unsettling her, driving her crazy, was the senseless death of a good person. People got killed by drunk drivers every day, but she'd never expected to have it happen to someone she knew.

Of all Jami's friends, Tracey had been the most ambitious. She'd been in her last year of medical school, and so filled with plans and hopes for her future. Tracey had been one of the sweetest, most decent people Jami had ever known. Perhaps that was why they hadn't been very close, Jami mused bitterly. She and Tracey were not very much alike.

And perhaps that was the hardest thing to accept. If anyone deserved to live, it was Tracey. She would have made a real contribution to the world, of that Jami was sure. Tracey had brightened every life she had touched. In contrast, she, Jamaica McKenzie, had done very few worthwhile things in her twenty-seven years of existence. Yet she was alive and Tracey was dead.

Jami handed a twenty-dollar bill to the cabdriver when he pulled up in front of her building and didn't remember to wait for the change. She walked broodingly by the doorman without saying a word. In a matter of moments the plush elevator had delivered her to the door of the penthouse, and she quietly went inside the dark room.

Jami hit the switch to turn on the chandelier, and shimmering light from hundreds of tiny-faceted bulbs instantly illuminated the living room. As she glanced around, she

contemplated briefly the kind of person who would deco-
rate a room entirely in white. White walls, white ceiling,
white carpet, white furniture. She used to think it looked so
chic, but now it looked, well, just white. It wasn't really a
living room, but rather a stark and cold showplace.

She'd just tossed her purse on the coffee table by the door
when her eyes caught sight of a letter addressed to her. She
snatched it up and went over to sit on the thickly cushioned
sofa, her own white clothing blending perfectly with the
white upholstery.

Jami stared at the envelope in her hand, recognizing her
grandfather's bold, broad handwriting at once, although
she thought his penmanship looked a little more unsteady
than it had the last time he'd written to her. She took a deep
breath and ripped the envelope open. The letter was short
and to the point. She read it quickly once, then folded it and
put it in the envelope. A few minutes later, she took it out
and read it again. Sighing deeply, she carried it with her into
her bedroom and closed the door behind her.

For a moment she was shaken by the reflection that stared
at her from the full-size mirror on the back of her door. Oh,
on the surface she didn't look any different than she ever
had, she consoled herself. She was as well dressed as she always was; tonight she was wearing tight white satin slacks
with an oversize white lacy blouse that came down to the
middle of her thighs. Her white, four-inch sandals brought
her height up to an inch short of six feet. Her long blond
hair was swept off her face and held to one side by a gold
clip. Faultlessly manicured fingernails were accented with
pale coral polish. Regular, strenuous visits to a health club
had made her body toned and shapely.

To walk into any room and have everyone's head turn in
appreciation had always brought her immense pleasure before. Now, it felt like a mockery. There had to be more to
Jamaica McKenzie than beauty. Had anyone ever looked
behind her emerald-green eyes to find out? She didn't think
so. Even she had never really looked before. Maybe it was
time she did.

She turned away from the mirror and in seconds she'd stripped off all her clothes and slipped between the cool sheets on her bed. She lay there without moving for several minutes staring at the ceiling.

"Oh, Hank," she whispered brokenly in the dark room, using her grandfather's first name as she always had, "I hope you know what you're doing."

It took several hours for Jami to get her grandfather's letter out of her thoughts and drift off in a restless sleep.

"You're going to go where?" Jason McKenzie demanded, staring in disbelief at his daughter.

"I'm going to Montana to visit Hank," Jami repeated calmly.

"But Jami, darling," her mother said soothingly, "why would you want to go way out there right now?"

"I told you already," Jami muttered, rising from the breakfast table. "His letter said he hadn't been feeling well lately and there was something he wanted to discuss with me."

"Why can't you just telephone him?" Jason asked. "Why do you have to travel all the way across the United States just to discuss something with him?"

"Daddy, you know as well as I do that Hank hates using the phone," Jami reminded him. "Besides, who will it hurt if I go see him on the ranch? I think it will be good for me."

Her parents exchanged uneasy glances. Her mother was the first to speak.

"Jami, we know you've had a lot on your mind lately. Why do you want to go see Hank now? You've never been close to him."

Jami swallowed her exasperation. She hadn't expected them to understand or even agree with her decision. It had been fifteen years since she'd visited her grandfather's ranch. Her mother was right; she and Hank weren't very close. But there had been a time, when she'd been a child, that she'd spent an entire summer on Hank's ranch. She always remembered that as one of the happiest times of her childhood. She'd been treated like just another kid out there, not like some precious and fragile rich man's proud accomplishment. It had taken her some time to adjust, but once she had, she'd thrived on the ranch.

There existed the remotest possibility that she might find a sliver of that serenity and happiness again if she returned there. Anyway, Hank had never asked her for a single thing until now, and she wasn't about to let him down.

"I already called out there this morning and made the arrangements," Jami announced firmly. "Thanks for your concern and everything, but I'm going whether you two approve or not. My plane leaves tomorrow morning at eight."

"Jami, are you sure there isn't more to this than you're telling us?"

Her breath caught, and she hoped her voice wouldn't give her away. "Positive."

"How long will you be gone?"

"I don't know. I'll keep in touch." Jami kissed each of her parents lightly on the cheek. "I'll see you two later. I've got some shopping to do."

At least she hadn't lied about needing to go shopping, she thought as she took the elevator to the street level, although what she really wanted to do was get away from her parents' probing eyes. She wasn't sure why she hadn't told them about the rest of Hank's letter, but some inner warning signal had cautioned her against it.

She pushed that impulsive decision out of her mind and turned her thoughts to her trip. Her wardrobe was filled with all the best and most expensive designer clothes, but she had almost nothing that would be suitable to wear on a working cattle and horse ranch. She would take care of that problem today. And in about thirty hours, she would be at Hank's ranch in her new Western clothes, far, far away from New York City.

The thought was both thrilling and terrifying.

* * *

The butterflies that had been in her stomach the whole trip increased tenfold when the commercial jet landed in Billings, Montana. Hank had arranged to have his private plane take her from the airport to the ranch. In less than an hour, she would be face to face with her grandfather.

Jami strode slowly into the airport, searching the unfamiliar faces for a man she did not know but assumed would be waiting for her. When the crowd dispersed after a few minutes, she accepted the fact no one was there to meet her. Frowning, she walked to the information desk in the center of the small airport.

"Excuse me," she said to the neatly tailored woman behind the desk. "My name is Jami McKenzie, and my grandfather, Hank McKenzie, is supposed to have a private plane here to pick me up."

"Yes, Miss McKenzie," the woman said with a warm smile. "Just go out through Gate Four and you'll find it. I believe the pilot is waiting for you."

Jami thanked her and headed toward Gate Four, feeling somewhat annoyed. It would have been much more courteous if the pilot had had the decency to meet her inside the airport. She walked outside and was instantly greeted by a nippy Montana breeze that was much cooler than the New York wind she had left several hours ago. She was chilled, exhausted from two nearly sleepless nights in a row, and more than a little nervous about seeing Hank. She was certainly in no mood to deal with an insolent employee.

As she neared the small private plane, she noticed a man leaning casually against the metal ladder that led up into the plane, his arms folded across his chest. He wasn't looking in her direction, but toward the mountains that loomed in the distance off the nose of the plane. His thick, black hair was blowing every which way across eyes protected by mirrored aviation sunglasses.

Jami paused when she reached his side. He was a good four inches taller than she was in her new high-heeled boots.

As far as she could tell, he still wasn't aware of her presence.

"Excuse me," she said indignantly.

The pilot slowly turned his head and looked at her. "Yes?" he said, one eyebrow cocked haughtily above his sunglasses.

Jami could only stare at him. She hadn't noticed his strong, classic features before when he'd been facing away from her. Nor had she taken the time to appreciate his well-muscled body, as she found herself doing now. Despite the cool temperatures, only a navy blue T-shirt covered his massive chest, revealing forearms and biceps that she was sure had been toughened like steel from hard work and not from barbells. The T-shirt tapered down to clothe a trim waist and was tucked neatly into close-fitting jeans that molded his narrow hips and lean thighs. His boots were so well broken in they made her new ones look fraudulent.

Jami reluctantly lifted her eyes to his face. She could see her startled expression reflected in his dark lenses. She hated the feeling of being exposed and vulnerable, knowing he could see her thoughts through her eyes while she could not read his through his mirrored sunglasses.

She swallowed and struggled to regain her composure. She was shocked and more than a little embarrassed that a strange man, however good-looking, could take away her poise so easily. It wasn't something she was used to, by any means. Especially when the man was just a McKenzie employee.

She reminded herself of that fact again, and when she spoke, her voice was controlled, even though her head and heart were pounding traitorously. "I'm Jamaica McKenzie. I believe you're supposed to take me to my grandfather's ranch."

"Jamaica?" he questioned mockingly, one corner of his mouth curled in a smile.

"Miss McKenzie to you," she snapped. She'd been sensitive all her life about her uncommon first name, but it made her skin tingle to hear him say it so smoothly, almost like a physical caress.

"Right this way, Miss McKenzie," he drawled, straightening up and motioning toward the open hatch.

She took one step up the ladder before stopping and turning to face him. "What about my luggage?"

"What about it?"

Jami gritted her teeth. If this man was trying to get on her nerves, he was doing a fantastic job. "Don't you think you should go get it?" she said pointedly.

He shrugged. "I guess since you didn't bring it with you, I don't have much choice, do I?"

"No, you don't." Jami turned her back on him and marched up the ladder. How could her grandfather put up with a man who had an attitude like that?

Once inside, she looked around the plane with dismay. There were only two small seats cramped together in the main part of the plane, with little legroom. It was quite a switch from the first-class luxury she'd had on the commercial jet. Her gaze wandered to the cockpit, and she made her way through the low door that opened to the control area, where there were two more seats side by side. There was just a touch more legroom there, she noticed, and certainly a much better view. She sat in the copilot's seat and buckled herself in.

Only a few minutes had passed when Jami heard the pilot loading her luggage into the storage compartment of the plane, and none too gently, either. When she heard him come up the ladder, she realized she was holding her breath and felt foolish.

"Damn," she heard him mutter, obviously looking for her. "Jamaica?"

"What?" She forced herself not to turn to look at him.

"What the hell are you doing in here?" he asked, his presence filling the cockpit.

"I'm waiting for you. Can we please get going?"

She heard him take a deep breath, as if trying to control his temper. "We're not going anywhere until you get in the seating area where you belong."

"I belong wherever I want to be. And I want to be here."

"Don't push your luck, sweetheart," the pilot said impatiently. "I've already had a long day, and you're not making it any shorter."

"Then I suggest you close the hatch and get up here so we can take off."

Muttering another curse under his breath, the pilot finally complied. In minutes, they were airborne.

Jami relaxed a little once they were up in the clouds, and the man next to her remained silent. She tried to watch him out of the corner of her eye, but she was afraid he'd catch her, so most of the time she simply stared at his hands. He had strong, confident hands, and she was fascinated by the way they glided so smoothly over the instrument panel. She could tell by the roughness of his fingers that he'd done his share of work, but judging by the finesse he displayed handling the controls, she knew those hands could also be very gentle. Gentle and sure over a woman's body, she thought, and a smile formed on her lips.

"Penny for your thoughts," the pilot said, amusement clear in his voice.

Jami jumped guiltily and felt color seeping into her cheeks. Was this disturbing man a mind reader too?

"I was just enjoying the scenery," she stammered.

"Oh? All I see right now is a lot of white."

Jami cautiously looked around her. They were surrounded by clouds, and indeed all she could see in every direction was white. It reminded her of her parents' living room, and was just as exciting to look at. She decided silence was the best answer and willed her face to return to its normal color.

"Where did you get a name like Jamaica?" the pilot asked suddenly.

"My parents had their honeymoon in Jamaica," she recited almost mechanically. How many hundreds of times had she been asked that question? "And I was conceived there. So they named me Jamaica."

"I'm sure glad they didn't have their honeymoon in Timbuktu."

She grinned before she could stop herself and glanced at him. He looked incredibly handsome, with a smile making his otherwise stern features come alive. If only she could see his eyes. What color would they be? she wondered. Probably brown, since his hair was so dark.

"What's your name?" she asked. "I suppose it's something totally ordinary."

He flashed her another smile. "Brock."

"Brock?" she repeated smugly. "Brock is hardly a common name. I'd say you have no right to make fun of my name when you have a name like Brock."

"At least I'm not named after a country."

"At least I can go by the name Jami," she pointed out. "It seems like you're stuck with your whole name."

"Assuming Brock is my whole name."

"Oh, come on. What could Brock possibly be short for?"

"Maybe I'll just let you wonder about that one, Miss McKenzie," he said with mock politeness.

The tone of his voice grated on her. "Actually, I have better things to wonder about than your name," she informed him.

"Really? I wouldn't think a spoiled rich girl like you would have many things to keep her mind stimulated. This is probably a foolish question, but do you have a job in New York?"

"It's none of your business," she snapped.

"Pleading the fifth amendment only answers my question as affirmative."

"As a matter of fact, I do volunteer work with illiterate children and also with the elderly."

"That's commendable, but can hardly be considered a real job. After all, you probably only flit back and forth between your charities whenever you feel like it."

"Well, I happen to feel like it quite often." Not as often as she could, she thought, but she wouldn't admit that to him.

"Still, as I said, that isn't an honest-to-goodness job. Haven't you heard? Women are supposed to be liberated and independent these days."

"I am independent," she tossed back coldly. "Independently wealthy."

"No," he corrected her. "Your father is independently wealthy. You sponge off him."

Jami gasped at the bluntness of his words, knowing they stung because she couldn't deny their truth. She took a deep breath as she tried to regain some composure.

"How long have you worked for my grandfather?" she asked coolly, determined to turn the conversation around.

Brock shrugged. "What difference does that make?"

"Because it will give me an idea of how hard it will be to get you fired."

"I doubt you'll have much luck in that department, Miss McKenzie," he told her with a touch of amusement.

"We'll just see about that." Jami threw him another indignant look and was taken aback by his sudden apparently casual and relaxed attitude. She longed to snatch those damn glasses off his face so she could see what was going on in his mind. Maybe she had taken his remarks too seriously. Considering how pleased he seemed, perhaps he'd only been teasing her, baiting her for some reason.

She didn't know, and she didn't care to dwell on it. Despite what Brock had said, she did have important things to think about. Like her future. And if Hank had really meant what he'd said in his letter.

Jami didn't realize she'd dozed off until she awoke with a start, instantly knowing that something was wrong. It took her a minute to realize the sinking feeling in her stomach was being caused by the much too abrupt descent of the plane.

"What's going on?" she cried out in horror.

"Just hang on, sweetheart," Brock said grimly. "Hang on tight."

"But we're not going to—to...." She clung to the arms of the seat, unable to voice the unthinkable word.

"Crash?" he supplied for her.

"Yes! Are we?"

"Not if I can help it."

But they had long since left the protective height of the clouds, and the ground was rushing up to meet them with a speed that scared the heart out of her. The trees on the mountain below them were getting bigger and bigger. Jami had no doubt they were going to die. They were going too fast, too out of control to survive impact with the ground. She held her breath and squeezed her eyes tightly shut. If she was going to be killed, she didn't want to see it happen.

Then she had no more time to think about anything. The plane jolted with a mighty lurch as it crashed into the trees. She heard a piercing scream, but she wasn't sure the sound came from her throat, because it sounded so strange and far away.

And then the darkness from her closed eyes was suddenly replaced by inky blackness as she was knocked unconscious.

Two

The first thing Jami was aware of when she came to was a tremendous throbbing in her head. She groaned as she touched her tender forehead, and her fingers came away covered with blood. It took her several minutes to focus her eyes, and when at last she could, all she could see were pine branches pushed up against what remained of the plane's smashed windshield. Where in the world was she? What had happened?

She forced her head to the side, despite its pounding protests. There was a man in the pilot's seat—what was his name?—hunched forward against his seat belt, his head drooped forward on his chest.

As Jami gaped at him, suddenly everything came back to her. The brief flight, the rude pilot named Brock, the crash. Good God, the crash! How had she ever survived it? Yet, unless she was going crazy or heaven was a strange-looking place, she was indeed alive. But had Brock fared as well? The way his neck was angled forward, she thought it must be broken. His mirrored sunglasses had fallen off, but his eyes were closed. A strong feeling of despondency washed through her because he was dead and she would never get the chance to see what color his eyes were....

She didn't know how long she sat there staring at him while tears ran silently down her cheeks before he suddenly stirred. A deep moan escaped his lips, and miraculously he straightened his neck and leaned his head against the seat.

"Brock?" Her joy at his being alive made her fingers fumble with the release on her seat belt. Finally she got it loose and crouched next to his seat, her hands on his arm. "Brock?" she repeated earnestly.

He moaned again and turned his head toward her. Slowly he opened his eyes.

"They're blue," she whispered huskily.

"What?" Brock frowned, squinting at Jami. "What's blue?"

"Your eyes," she answered at once, too relieved to feel silly. She dropped her head against his strong shoulder as sobs shook her body. "Thank God you're all right."

She gave him a startled look when he pushed her away from him. "Try to pull yourself together and stop crying," he said gruffly. "Tears aren't going to help us now."

Jami's eyes widened at his stinging rejection, then narrowed as her temper was ignited in a defensive reaction. "Pardon me all to pieces!"

"How's your head?" he asked with a little less harshness.

"I'll survive." She stood and walked on shaky legs into the main compartment of the plane to escape Brock's unyielding gaze. "What happened, anyway? Why did we crash?"

Brock released his own seat belt. He ducked through the cockpit door and trailed after Jami. "I wish I knew," he said, a frown furrowing his brow. "The engine just conked out."

Jami shook her head, ignoring the ache that intensified with every movement. "We're lucky to be alive," she said, still in awe of that fact.

"Luck had very little to do with it, sweetheart. If I wasn't such a damn good pilot, we would be dead right now."

"If you don't mind, I'll save my congratulations until we get to my grandfather's ranch. What do we do now, Mr. Damn Good Pilot?" she asked with mock sweetness.

"How about getting some fresh air? It's getting a little stuffy in here," he muttered.

Jami stepped back, and Brock opened the door. A brisk wind blasted them in the face, and Jami shivered as Brock dropped the ladder.

"Come on, I'll help you down," he offered grudgingly, reaching for her arm.

"I can manage on my own, thanks just the same." She jerked her arm away, moved past him and went down the first few steps of the ladder. When she was almost to the bottom, she stopped.

"What's the matter?" Brock asked from behind her.

"The ladder doesn't reach all the way to the ground." She eyed the broken pine branches resting under the ladder. She wasn't feeling steady enough on her feet to attempt a jump onto possibly uneven footing. "It looks like there might be a drop from here, but I can't tell for sure."

"Here, let me get by you."

Jami pushed herself against the railing to make room for him to squeeze around her. As he did, he put his hands on her shoulders, and for a moment his whole brawny body was pressed against the length of her. The tingling effect of the contact made her knees even weaker, and she shivered uncontrollably again, only this time it wasn't from the stiff breeze. Her fingers curled around the railing in a death grip, the cold steel giving her much needed strength. She closed her eyes and took a deep, stabilizing breath, willing herself to keep her mind on her present situation and off of other foolishness.

"Jami?"

Her eyes flew open and met Brock's questioning gaze. He was standing below her with both hands held out.

"Come on, it's not very far. I'll help you."

She nodded and stepped to the bottom rung of the ladder. Brock grasped her lightly around her waist and swung her easily to the ground. She stumbled a little as her feet tried to find a level place to stand, and he gripped her tighter.

"Are you okay?" he asked softly, his face so close to hers that she could feel his warm breath like a gentle caress on her cheeks.

"I'm scared to death," she whispered, and that much was true, but she hoped Brock didn't know what was scaring her. For as much as she realized how grave their predicament was, she was even more terrified of how acutely her body was reacting to him. More than anything at that moment, she wished she could get away from him and pull herself together.

Brock fought the instinctive urge he had to comfort her. He needed her to be strong as much as he needed to keep himself clearheaded and distant. "Here," he said, lightly taking her elbow and steering her a few feet away from the plane. "Hold up this tree while I check out the damage."

She leaned against the bumpy pine tree's trunk without a word. The sharp bark poked uncomfortably into her back, but she barely noticed it. She kept her eyes focused on Brock until he disappeared around the side of the plane. He soon returned, and after a quick glance at her, he stepped to the ladder again.

"Maybe you should go inside now," he suggested. He'd found the fuel line intact, so he was sure the plane was in no danger of blowing up. "It's cold out here, and I don't want you going into shock on me. I want to look around some more."

He should help her, he thought as he watched her climb wearily up the ladder. He felt like a louse for not reassuring her when she so obviously needed it, but he had to keep some space between them. Brock ached to hold her, as unwilling as he was to admit it. Damn it, he had never in his life had any woman affect him the way she did. And it made no sense at all, because before the crash the only thing he'd found to like about her was her looks.

Yes, Hank's granddaughter was certainly easy on the eyes. Thank God for his aviator sunglasses, or she'd have seen his gaze roaming all over her when she'd marched up to the plane. He'd seen her right away of course, although he'd pretended otherwise. How could he possibly not notice her? Her slim figure, wind-blown blond hair and flashing green eyes were enough to make any man gape. But her attitude—that was another story.

He'd expected Hank's granddaughter to reek of money— he knew the kind of life she led—but he hadn't anticipated her being quite so uppity. Hank was so down-to-earth, so honest and decent, it was hard to believe the two were related.

She didn't belong here, plain and simple. Unless he could convince either Hank or Jami of that, an old man's dreams would be shattered, and Brock's future would be affected, as well. Maybe if he reminded himself of that often enough, he could control the crazy attraction he felt whenever he looked at her.

For when her frightened and vulnerable green eyes met his, his stomach turned to mush. Not to mention what happened to other parts of his anatomy. He usually preferred to abstain from casual sex, but he had to wonder if he should make an exception in Jami's case. Then he almost laughed at himself. She thought he was a lowly cowhand. She wouldn't touch him with a ten foot pole. Well, if she wanted to think he was just another McKenzie employee, that was fine with him. When she found out who he really was, it would be worth the sacrifice.

As he carefully circled the plane again, he had a smile on his face.

Inside the plane, Jami was far from smiling. Their situation was just starting to sink in, and she was trying very hard not to give in to the panic that threatened to take over her normally rational mind. How far were they from Hank's ranch? she wondered. They must've been flying at least half an hour before they went down, although she couldn't be sure because she'd fallen asleep—for ten minutes? Maybe fifteen? Brock must know exactly where they were, since he'd been piloting the plane. And surely there must be some emergency provisions in the plane, so they'd have something to eat until they were rescued or reached help on their own. Brock must know how to survive in the wilderness. What man who lived in this remote and desolate area of the country wouldn't?

Jami sighed and gently massaged her aching temples. It wasn't until she felt the stickiness there that she remembered she'd been bleeding earlier. After searching the airplane floor for a few moments, she finally located her purse and withdrew a small compact from it. She winced as she examined her face in the tiny round mirror. There was a nasty-looking cut above her right eye that had left a trail of now-dried blood all the way down her cheek. A bruise was already turning bright shades of purple in the middle of her forehead, and she had a small cut on her nose.

"You certainly won't win any beauty pageants looking like this," she said to her reflection. She walked to the back of the plane, pulled open a door and to her relief found a bathroom. It wasn't any bigger than her parents' linen closet, but it was better than nothing. The mirror that had been over the sink was shattered, but at least she had her compact. She grabbed a towel off the floor and turned the handle on the faucet. Nothing.

She sighed again and sat on the closed toilet. Why should she care how she looked, anyway? But she couldn't quite fool herself into thinking that it didn't matter to her what Brock thought. Still, it irritated her that she was being such an idiot. The way Brock had talked to her before the crash shouldn't have left any doubt in her mind about his feelings for her. And his abruptness with her when she'd been crying said plenty, too. In fact, he was probably plotting right now to leave her here alone.

That thought was so disturbing that she didn't even hear Brock's footsteps as he climbed up the ladder. She jumped when she heard him call out her name in an alarmed voice.

"I'm in here," she said quietly.

"Oh." He sounded relieved. She heard him rustling around in the cockpit before he approached the bathroom. "Are you all right?" he asked hesitantly.

"Sure." She got up and stood in the doorway, her arms crossed over her chest. "What's the verdict?"

"The radio didn't survive, but luckily the fuel tank did, so you should be perfectly safe here while I go for help."

"Forget it," she scoffed immediately, putting aside the instant pang of disappointment his words brought. "There's no way I'm going to stay here by myself while you go traipsing off around the countryside."

"You'll be safer here," he said sternly. "It isn't Park Avenue out there, you know. It's rough country, and you aren't equipped to handle it. Besides, there's a good chance someone will come looking for us, and they might spot the plane."

"Then we can both wait here to be rescued."

Brock shook his head. "We can't count on that happening. We'll increase our odds tenfold if I head for Hank's ranch on my own."

"I won't stay here alone."

"Stop being so naive and spoiled for a minute and listen to reason!" Brock exploded, unable to control his temper any longer. He hadn't expected her to agree to stay behind, but he'd thought it was at least worth a try. He wasn't looking forward to dragging her along with him, and it would probably be a whole lot less complicated if she stayed in the plane. "Why can't you get it through your thick head that this is for your own good?"

"I'll decide what's for my own good, thank you!"

Brock crossed the few steps through the plane that took him to within inches of Jami's tense body. "You want to come with me?" he asked, his blazing eyes boring into hers.

"Yes!"

"Do you have any idea what you'll be up against if you do?"

Jami wished she could back up into the bathroom. He was too close, and a sudden wave of dizziness swept through her. She could feel her pulse pounding in her neck, matching time with the throbbing in her forehead. Still she stood her ground. "I'm sure there wouldn't be anything I couldn't handle."

"Oh, really? Can you handle mountain lions? Rattlesnakes? A five-thousand-foot climb in altitude? Thick brush and thorny bushes? A minimum of food and water? Can you handle this?" Brock reached out and roughly pulled her into his arms and in the next instant had brought his mouth crushingly down on hers.

He certainly hadn't planned to kiss her, and the last thing in the world he expected her to do was respond, but after the initial shock wore off, he felt her hungrily matching his own fervor as they devoured each other's lips. It wasn't until he realized his lungs were fighting for air that he released her, and they both stood for several minutes eyeing each other almost warily until their ragged breathing returned to near normal.

"Can you handle all that, Jami?" Brock asked, his voice husky and his eyes smoldering.

Jami didn't know what surprised her more—Brock kissing her or her intense response. He had shaken her to the core, and she knew by the satisfied look on his face that he knew it too. It was that smug smirk he was wearing that proved her undoing. She shoved him backwards.

Brock caught his balance as he ran into the passenger seats. He straightened and looked at her speculatively. "Maybe I deserved that, and maybe I didn't. I don't recall you struggling while I was kissing you."

"Now, you listen to me," she said deliberately, pointing an accusing finger at him. "I am going with you, and under no circumstances will you repeat what just happened, or I swear I'll make up such fantastic stories to tell my grand-

father when we get back that he'll shoot you personally! Is
that understood?''

He shook his head, clearly amused. ''Anything you say,
Miss McKenzie. I promise not to kiss you again unless I ask
for your permission and you grant it.''

''Don't hold your breath.''

''Now that you've laid out your ground rules, I have some
of my own,'' he told her in a steadfast voice that left no
room for argument. ''While we're out there in the wilderness, we'll just be two people, a man and a woman. No airs,
no attitudes, no threats, no orders, no complaining. Is that
understood?''

Jami returned his hard gaze for a moment before she answered him. ''That's fine with me so long as it's a two-way
street.''

''Meaning?''

''Meaning I don't want any more insults or insolence or
threats or orders, either. Deal?''

Brock flashed her a boyish grin that relaxed his stern features. The lady did have spunk. ''Deal. But before we do
anything else, I want to take a look at your head. Come over
here and sit down.''

She stiffened immediately. ''I'm fine.''

''Let me be the judge of that.'' He motioned to one of the
passenger seats. ''Sit down.''

''I thought we just agreed you weren't going to order me
around.''

He smiled innocently. ''Please sit down.''

She glared at him as she finally complied. Her glare
melted instantly when his gentle fingers brushed aside her
bangs. She kept her attention on his chest, unable to meet
his eyes when he was just a breath away.

''I can't tell how deep the cut is with all that dried blood
on it.'' He stood and headed toward the bathroom.

''Don't bother. I already checked the sink. No water came
out of the faucet.''

He paused in the doorway, a thoughtful frown creasing his forehead before he suddenly winked at her. "Well, there's one other place there might be some water."

She leaned into the aisle to watch him. He lifted the lid on the toilet seat and snapped his fingers.

"Bingo."

Her eyes widened in disbelief. "You want to wash my face with water from a toilet bowl?"

"Why not? It's clean."

"You've got to be kidding."

"Look, lady, I didn't say you had to drink it." He dipped a towel into the bowl and wrung it out, then stood in front of her again. "Besides, think how much better you'll look without all that blood on you."

She edged away from him. "Trying to appeal to my sense of vanity isn't going to get you anywhere."

"Then how about if I appeal to your common sense? I need to see how bad that wound is, and I can't do it any other way." He squatted so he was at eye level with her. "Now, be a good girl and hold still."

She gritted her teeth and stared at the towel as it got closer and closer to her face. "I owe you for this one."

His grin was maddening. "A simple thank you will suffice." He meticulously scrubbed her face, being extra careful around the bruise. He was relieved to see the cut wasn't serious. "You can stop glowering at me. I'm done."

"So, will I live?"

He nodded. "You'll probably have some headaches the next few days, but it could have been a lot worse." He tossed the towel on the floor. "Now, Miss McKenzie, it's time to scrape together some supplies so we can start our little journey."

In less than an hour, they were on their way. Brock had gathered all the supplies he could make use of and bound them in a blanket that served as a makeshift backpack. After a short, heated debate, he'd finally relented to Jami bringing along the overnight bag that had been inside one of her suitcases, as long as she made room for the first-aid kit among her various toiletries and change of clothes. He'd also insisted that she leave behind her new designer cowboy boots and wear her broken-in tennis shoes instead.

And so they'd set out, Brock leading the way in his leather flight jacket, a compass in his hand and the blanket of supplies on his back. Jami trailed after him, wearing the warmest coat she'd brought along, with her overnight bag and an empty canteen slung over her shoulder.

"Are you sure we shouldn't have stayed in the plane until morning and then started out fresh?" Jami called out to Brock an hour and a half after they left. The sun was getting low in the sky, and already her shoulder ached from toting the unaccustomed weight over less than favorable terrain. She was tired, more than a little hungry, and despite the cool temperature, she could feel a thin trickle of sweat dripping between her shoulder blades. Brock, however, looked like he was on a casual stroll through Central Park.

"There was no sense wasting three hours of light sitting back at the plane." He stopped and turned to watch her increasingly slow progress as she caught up to him, and he cursed under his breath. He knew she was doing her best, and she hadn't complained yet, but at this rate it would take them a week to make their way. "You're anxious to get to Hank's ranch, aren't you?" he asked as she stopped next to him.

Jami nodded, afraid to speak while she was short of breath, because she didn't want him to know how tired she was. Why did he have to look like he could go on like this all night when she felt like she could hardly take another ten steps?

"Are you thirsty?"

"A little." Actually, her throat was so dry she'd barely been able to swallow for the past half hour. "The canteen's empty, though, remember?"

"It won't be for long. See that patch of dark green brush and that thick grove of trees at the end of this meadow?"

She sighed involuntarily. The area Brock was pointing to looked five miles away. "Yes, I see it."

"There should be some kind of stream coming off the mountain. If there is, we'll make camp for the night. Unless, of course, you'd rather start up that mountain tonight," he said, his voice light and teasing.

She glared at him until the full meaning of his words sank in, then the expression on her face changed from irritation to despair. "You mean that's where we have to go tomorrow?"

"I'm afraid so. If we don't travel as the crow flies, it would take us a month to get to Hank's ranch. His spread is on the other side of these mountains. Lucky for you, his place isn't in the big mountain ranges west of here, or we'd probably never make it. The few mountains that are between us and Hank's ranch are half the size of those beauties." He motioned toward the vast Rockies, visible as shadowy forms against the horizon.

She shuddered, realizing things could be worse. "But aren't there any other ranches between here and Hank's?" she asked hopefully.

"No. This is Montana, not New York. People live more than three feet apart out here."

"Thanks for the geography lesson," she said tartly. "Let's get going. I'd rather keep walking than stand here and get into an argument with you."

"My sentiments exactly," he muttered.

As she trudged along behind Brock through waist-deep grass and weeds and wildflowers, Jami realized the terrain they had crossed so far that day was probably the easiest they would cover. It had taken them about twenty minutes to work their way out of the thick but fragrant grove of pine trees once they'd left the plane. After that, they'd gone through a couple of small, grassy clearings before reaching the huge meadow they were now in. The going so far hadn't been all that tough, except she had to constantly watch the footing in front of her because the ground was cluttered with rocks, dead branches, and viny plants that grabbed hold of her shoes. But climbing that mountain was going to be something else entirely.

She shifted her overnight bag and the canteen from one aching shoulder to the other for the twentieth time. Lifting her gaze from the ground to check on their progress, she saw they still had a long way to go. At least Brock had slowed down a little, she noticed with relief. She was sure it was solely for her benefit. She smiled smugly as she thought about how enjoyable it would be to plop him down in the middle of Grand Central Station during rush hour, or Time's Square on New Year's Eve, and see how well he got around out of his natural element.

By keeping her mind busy plotting other such dastardly situations to put Brock in, before Jami knew it, they reached the end of the meadow. In minutes Brock located a clear, swift-moving stream about four feet wide. She shrugged the overnight bag and canteen off her shoulder and sank gratefully to the ground at the bank of the creek.

Brock smiled at her eagerness. "Don't drink too much too fast," he warned.

Not taking the time to fill the canteen first, Jami bent over the stream and scooped some of the ice-cold water from her curled-up hand into her mouth. After she took a few refreshing swallows, she turned to Brock. "I'm not totally ignorant about everything, you know," she informed him. "I used to work out a lot at a health club, and I know all about how to drink after exercise."

Brock's grin only deepened. "I think this is a little different than a New York health spa, don't you?"

"Maybe. But the principle is the same." She looked at him out of the corner of her eye while she continued to drink. She had never imagined plain water could taste so good. If Brock wasn't gawking at her, she could savor it a lot more. "Aren't you thirsty?" she finally asked in frustration. "Or are cowboys like camels and don't need water?"

"Oh, I'm thirsty all right," he admitted with a chuckle. "But right now I'm getting a bigger kick out of watching you drink."

"Why?"

"Well, I'm just trying to imagine you in some fancy gown at a big party, sipping Perrier in a New York penthouse." His blue eyes sparkled mischievously. "You have to admit it's quite a contrast to the mussed-up woman I see right now with creek water dripping down her chin."

Her hand immediately went up to wipe off her face, and Brock burst out in laughter.

"Need a cocktail napkin?" he quipped between chortles.

She grabbed the canteen and thrust it into the stream until it was partly filled. Then she jumped to her feet and in three steps was standing in front of Brock.

He eyed the canteen being threateningly waved in his face. "What do you think you're going to do with that?"

"I'm going to see what you look like with water dripping all over you!" She raised the canteen over his head.

Brock snatched it from her hand. "Here, I'll save you the trouble." He threw his head back and dumped the entire contents of the canteen on his face. When it was empty, he shook his head several times, and water from his thick black hair sprayed in all directions.

"There, how's that?" he asked, a wide grin enlivening his rugged features. "I hope you enjoyed it, because it sure felt great to me."

His light mood combined with the sudden realization of the absurdity of the whole situation caused the tension and anger in her to melt away. She had no choice but to laugh.

"That's better," Brock said in approval when their laughter had died down. "If we can't keep our sense of humor while we're out here, we've had it."

She supposed he was right, even though she'd never been one to laugh at herself. Still, she'd come to Hank's ranch in hopes of changing her life, and maybe this was a small but positive step.

"Well, I for one am going to take advantage of this stream by cleaning up," Brock said a few minutes later, breaking what had fast been becoming an awkward silence between them. After they'd stopped laughing, they didn't know what to say to each other.

She'd forgotten that she must be a mess. "Good idea," she mumbled, turning from him.

"You can stay here, and I'll go downstream past that bend so we can both have a little privacy."

"Okay." She watched him move gracefully around trees and bushes until he was out of sight. He's so at home out here, she thought with a touch of envy. She, on the other hand, had never felt so lost and uneasy. She didn't like having to depend on Brock for everything. What would she do if something happened to him? She would die out here, of that she had no doubt.

She tried to push her worries out of her mind as she dug through her overnight bag in search of some soap, a brush and her compact. She finally found everything she needed and was soon scrubbing off the last evidence of their crash except the tender purplish bruise that brightly adorned her forehead. Unable to wash it away, she did the next best thing; she covered it up by carefully brushing her bangs across it. Now if only the wind wouldn't blow until the bruise went away, she'd be all right. She knew there wasn't much chance of that happening, but she still felt immensely better for the moment knowing she was clean, her hair was brushed until it was soft and silky again, and her face didn't look like she'd just been in a boxing ring. Once all that was accomplished, she filled the canteen and drank deeply from it.

She was leaning against a tree at the bank of the stream when she heard Brock making his way back. At least she hoped it was Brock. What if it was some wild animal? Her heart started thumping crazily in her chest, and she realized she was holding her breath as she sat in frozen terror.

Suddenly the rustling stopped. "Jami?" Brock's deep voice called out.

Her breath was expelled in a quick blast. Now if she could only stop shaking. "It's okay, I'm decent."

Brock heard the quiver in her voice and was at her side in seconds. "Are you all right?"

She forced a smile. "I'm fine. Why?"

"You sounded, well, funny," he stammered, feeling a little foolish. She did look fine. Better than fine, in fact. She looked more like the polished and beautiful woman who had met him at the plane in the Billings airport just a few short hours ago.

Except she wasn't the same woman, not by a long shot. That woman had been confident and haughty and proud. The woman who sat before him now had a much different look in her eyes. He could see fear and uneasiness, and something else he couldn't quite put his finger on. He felt inexplicably disturbed, seeing her like this.

Jami squirmed nervously at his solemn scrutiny of her. Anxious to get his mind on something other than her, she finally got up the courage to ask him the one thing that had been bothering her since they'd left the plane.

"How far are we from my grandfather's ranch?" She'd carried the dreaded question with her all this way, but she couldn't keep from asking it any longer. She knew the answer would be discouraging, but after getting a taste of what their journey would be like, she had to know.

He hesitated for a moment, wondering if he should tell her the truth. He decided it was best to be honest. "About fifty miles, give or take a mile or two."

"Oh." She wasn't sure if that was good news or bad. "How many miles did we go today?"

He shrugged. "Three, four at the most."

"That's all?" It had felt more like twenty.

"We only walked for two hours," he pointed out. "Starting first thing in the morning, we'll be walking all day. Although the going will be a lot slower for awhile."

"So how many days do you think it will take us?"

"Oh, I'd say four days, maybe five. That is, if the weather stays nice, and we don't have any other unexpected problems."

"Unexpected problems? Like what?"

"I told you what we'd be up against before we left the plane, remember?"

She sighed. "I was hoping you were exaggerating."

"Sorry, sweetheart, I didn't exaggerate one bit," he told her, his voice more harsh than he intended. He wanted to shake her, to shake all the fear and meekness right out of her body. Then it suddenly came to him that the biggest reason he hated seeing her like this was that it was bringing out unwanted feelings in him. Feelings of protectiveness, sympathy and caring. And caring about this woman would be disastrous. He shook his head and reminded himself why she was there.

He'd been Mr. Nice Guy since they'd left the plane, and that had gone on too long. He decided he needed to pick a fight with her. Maybe it would bring back some of the spark in her eyes, and he hoped it would also serve to put some distance between them.

"Why did you come out here in the first place? It's obvious you have no great love for this kind of country," he said, forced contempt in his voice.

Jami glanced at him sharply, once more stung by his sudden change in attitude for no apparent reason. "I happen to think Montana is a beautiful state."

"Yeah, a nice place to visit and all that, right?"

"What difference could it possibly make to you, anyway?"

Brock almost smiled at her defensive and hostile tone. He knew it wouldn't be hard to get in an argument with her. She already looked more like her old self, and he was feeling better, too. "I've known your grandfather for a long time, and I've never seen you out here before. How long has it been since you've seen Hank?"

She hesitated, knowing the truth didn't sound good. But he probably already knew the answer, so it didn't seem worth it to lie. "About fifteen years," she finally told him flatly.

"So why after fifteen years do you suddenly decide to come visit good old Gramps?"

"Hank asked me to come," she said simply.

"Why?"

"It's none of your damn business why!"

"Everything about you is my business as long as we're out here."

She glared at him in outrage, only too aware of the full meaning of his statement. "All you're doing is finishing the job my grandfather gave you to do, only now you're doing it on the ground instead of in the air. Either way, you're not entitled to any special rights. My business is still my business and absolutely none of yours."

"Is that right?" Brock turned his head to look at her, one eyebrow raised. "And what if I decided that no job was worth this hassle and left you out here to fend for yourself? I could make it back to the ranch in half the time by myself."

Her emerald eyes stopped spitting fire and widened in sudden fear. "You wouldn't do that," she said, her voice no more than a whisper.

"How do you know I wouldn't?"

Jami could only stare at him, trying to figure out whether he was serious, but his stony face gave away nothing. Really, how did she know he wouldn't do such an awful thing? He certainly looked like an irresponsible rogue. She knew nothing about this man, not even his last name, for heaven's sake. How did she know how trustworthy he was? She looked away from his steady gaze and shivered as she stared unseeingly at the bubbling water rushing over the gray rocks in front of her.

Brock's chest tightened as if a giant fist was trying to squeeze the breath out of him. He hadn't meant to scare her so much, but he'd had no idea she would take his words seriously. And now she'd returned to her state of nervous timidity, and he felt, well, he felt like hell. He reached out to grasp her shoulder reassuringly, and when she cringed, he let go. "Jami?" he said gently.

She refused to acknowledge him.

"Jami, look at me. Please."

When she at last turned to face him, his heart stopped with a thud as he saw the unshed tears illuminating her large green eyes. He reached out again and ever so tenderly pulled her unprotesting body into his arms.

"I'm sorry if I frightened you. I thought you'd know I was just kidding," he said softly as he stroked her hair.

She let him hold her for a moment before she pulled away, sat down and leaned against a tree. She felt a little silly for letting his harsh words get to her as they had, because she knew somehow that this man would not abandon her. And being held in his arms certainly confirmed that feeling.

"I know now," she said when she was in control of herself.

It bothered him that she could think he was the kind of man who would leave a helpless woman alone in the wilderness. "Hey, I may not particularly like your being here, but I'm no monster, either. You can trust me."

"I'm counting on that."

"Besides, I promised Hank I'd take good care of you." Brock flashed her a grin, hoping to lighten up what had become a solemn conversation.

Jami eyed him quizzically, opting to join him in his levity. "How good?" she asked with mock suspicion.

"The best." He winked at her. "After all, how many pilots you've flown with took the time to give you a personal guided tour through their state's most beautiful scenery?"

She laughed. "Only one."

Brock squeezed her knee briefly, and his face sobered. "You don't have to worry, Jami. I'll make sure you get to your grandfather's ranch safe and sound. You have my word."

She could only nod, as a lump had formed in her throat when he'd touched her. She believed Brock would get her to the ranch sound. But safe? Would she ever feel safe again with him around to play such havoc with her senses? If one reassuring pat could render her speechless, what kind of shape would she be in after spending four or five days with this man?

Three

———

Dinner that night was a simple affair, with pork and beans, beef jerky and coffee. Brock had told her to get used to that as their menu, since there hadn't been much else stored in the plane. Still, it was food, and once it had been heated over a blazing camp fire, Jami devoured her share quickly. The coffee, however, was another story. It was so strong it burned all the way from her throat to her stomach.

"I've never been much of a coffee drinker," she admitted to Brock as she continued to sip the thick brew out of a metal cup. "If I had to drink this kind all the time, I'd probably give it up for life."

Brock chuckled as he watched her from across the fire. The warmth had made her pale cheeks rosy, and she looked more relaxed than he'd seen her all day. "It is a little strong, even for me. But it's better than nothing."

Jami stifled a yawn. Although coffee usually kept her awake, she felt very sleepy all of a sudden. Darkness had enshrouded them a short time ago, and when the sun disappeared it had left damp, chilly air in its place. She drank the coffee as slowly as she could, more to preserve the heated cup that felt so good in her cold hands than because of the unpleasant taste.

"Just how low does the temperature get at night this time of year?" she asked with a trace of reluctance. It was another question she felt she was really better off not knowing the answer to, but she could only worry about it in ignorance for so long. She had goose bumps all over her body and would have given almost anything for a wool hat.

"The low fifties, if we're lucky. The fire should keep us warm enough, though. And you can have the blanket."

She smiled at him. "Chivalry is alive and well in Montana."

He liked the way the flames caught the light in her eyes and made them sparkle at him. The fire also did wonderful things for her long hair, giving it bright gold highlights that nearly matched the color of the flames. Careful, he warned himself. Staring at her wasn't very smart.

He reached over and took the coffee cup from her hands. "I'll rinse these out and pick things up. Why don't you turn in? You look beat. You've had quite a day today, but tomorrow will be even worse."

"I don't see how it could be." What could top crashing in an airplane? It hardly seemed possible that this morning she had been in New York. It felt like months since she had been anywhere other than where she was right now.

She smiled gratefully as Brock handed her their only blanket. She curled herself into a tight little ball and tucked the blanket up under her chin. She wished she could move closer to the warmth of the fire, but Brock had warned her earlier about sleeping far enough away from it so an errant spark wouldn't make her into a human torch.

Jami closed her eyes and listened to the comforting sound of Brock rambling around their campsite. When she'd first thought about spending their nights together in these conditions, she had doubted she would ever get a wink of sleep. But she had worried needlessly. She was so exhausted from the day's ordeal that in a matter of minutes she was deliciously oblivious to everything but her pleasant dreams of sleeping under a thick quilt on a warm water bed.

It seemed she'd barely closed her eyes before they popped open in instant alertness. Some strange sound had awakened her, but nearly a minute passed before she heard it again. It was a howl, or a call, or a challenge. She didn't know what it was, but it was definitely from an animal, and it was definitely loud. And it had to be close.

She fought to remain calm, and reminded herself that wild animals were afraid of fire. But the camp fire had burned down so all that remained were a few small, glowing pieces of spitting wood, and she wasn't sure that was enough of a threat to keep the creature away.

A few feet beyond the circle of the fire she could make out the outline of Brock's body. He was sleeping peacefully, his face turned away from her. Let him sleep, she told herself. If she woke him up, he'd be mad as hell and hardly sympathetic. In fact, he'd undoubtedly jeer at her cowardice and berate her up and down. The animal was probably a lot farther away than it sounded. Most likely, it was miles and miles. . . .

But when she heard another howl, she couldn't help herself. Every hair on her body was standing on end, and her heart was racing so fast she felt like she'd just run a marathon. Having Brock upset with her for ruining his sleep was preferable to being eaten alive.

"Brock?" Her voice came out in a whispered squeak. "Are you awake?"

She heard him sigh and felt instantly more secure. "I am now. What is it?"

"That's what I was hoping you would tell me," she said with a shudder. "Didn't you hear that animal? It sounded so close."

With a muttered grunt, Brock rolled over to face her and sat up. "That animal was a coyote. A harmless coyote. And I would guess he's two miles from here."

"Two miles?" Jami sat up and shook her head, the loud and eerie call clear in her memory. "It had to be closer than that."

"Their calls carry easily on a clear night. Believe me, you'd have known if he was any closer. He would have been twice as loud."

She edged unconsciously toward the glowing embers. "Shouldn't you build up the fire a little bit?"

"What for?" He raised one eyebrow. "Are you cold?"

"Yes," she answered, much too quickly.

For a long time, he simply sat there, his eyes traveling over her, and she was certain he wasn't going to comply. But then he shook his head and got up to get more wood. In minutes he had the flames blazing as the fire eagerly devoured the dry timber. Satisfied, he sat down where he'd been sleeping.

Jami wrapped the blanket around her shoulders and gazed at Brock's face as the flames alternately brightened then shadowed his chiseled features. It was odd that at times the fire accented the harshness of his face, making him look almost cruel, then the next instant it was softening it, to make him look kind and gentle. The alternating changes fascinated her as much as the man himself did.

"Why are you looking at me like that?" he asked curiously as he saw the tension slip away from her to be replaced by—what? Longing?

She smiled almost shyly, which further disarmed him. "Thank you for getting the fire going again."

He winked at her and tipped an imaginary cowboy hat over his eyes. "My pleasure, ma'am. Now you better try to get back to sleep. Morning's only a few hours away."

She would've liked to keep talking to him, but a sudden wave of exhaustion swam through her. In fact, she could hardly keep her eyes open. She lay down and repositioned the blanket over herself.

"Were you cold before that coyote woke you up?" she asked sleepily.

"What?" The coyote hadn't awakened him; she had. But that was beside the point. "Why?"

She yawned. She was pretty sure the coyote was far away by now. Still, Brock seemed far away, too. "I kind of feel sorry for you with no blanket. I was going to offer to share mine with you if you're cold."

It was the last thing he expected her to say. The offer was mighty tempting, and it had little to do with him being cold. "Do I only get to share the blanket, or can I share your body heat, too?"

Her eyes flew open to gauge the seriousness of his words. He was grinning teasingly. She closed her eyes again. She thought she would be able to sleep alone, but the idea of him next to her was oddly appealing. "Actually, I was hoping to share some of your body heat. I feel so chilled right now."

"Even though I stoked the fire?"

"All right, so I had ulterior motives for asking you to do that." Her voice dropped to a chagrined murmur. "I just want to feel safe for the rest of the night. So how about it?"

He couldn't refuse her even if he'd wanted to. "What happened to my independent city girl?" he asked flippantly as he stretched out alongside her.

"I'll be independent again tomorrow," she mumbled sleepily. "When it's light out."

He smiled and pulled part of the blanket over himself. It felt good having her so close. Too good. But for the rest of the night he wasn't going to think about it. "Jami?" he whispered into her ear.

"Hmm?"

A dozen different things he wanted to say battled inside him. In the end, he settled for the easy way out. "Good night."

She sighed and snuggled against him. In the morning she'd probably be horrified that she'd slept with him like this. He was, after all, little more than a stranger. But for now she was too tired to care because it felt so wonderful. "Good night. Sleep well."

As he listened to her deep, even breathing, Brock wondered if she was kidding. Despite his better judgment, he
curled one arm around her waist and brought her body close
to his. It was with supreme effort that he was able to lay
there without moving against her or letting his hand roam.

Sleep well? he thought with a silent groan. If he slept at
all, he'd be damn lucky.

The sun was just starting to warm the day when Jami
awoke. As she opened her eyes to the sight of Brock's chest,
she realized why she'd felt so safe and warm as she'd drifted
from sleep to consciousness. Sometime during the last few
hours, she'd turned around. One of Brock's arms was
tucked under her head, and the other was wrapped protec-
tively around her back.

She smiled slightly and buried her nose in Brock's T-shirt
one last time. It felt good to wake up with a man, she
thought blissfully. She hadn't done that since she'd been
engaged to Jonathon, and that had been three years ago.
Jonathon. His name brought a bitter taste to her mouth
even now. It also served to remind her that she had enjoyed
Brock's embrace long enough. Still, it was with reluctance
that she started to squirm quietly out of his arms.

She didn't get far. As soon as she'd moved an inch,
Brock's grip tightened. She glanced at his face, but he appeared to be sleeping. She wiggled around some more, and
finally he stirred and loosened his hold on her. Before she
could get away, his pale blue eyes had opened and were
boring into hers.

"Good morning," he said in a deep voice that was raspy
from sleep.

Jami felt her cheeks flush. "Good morning yourself."

"Sleep well?"

"Yes. And you?"

"Like a baby," he lied. He hadn't fallen asleep until
about an hour before dawn. It had taken him that long to
calm himself down. Having her shapely body pressed
against him had given almost more torture than pleasure.

"So," she quipped, "when will the champagne brunch be served?"

He chuckled as he rolled onto his back and stretched his arms over his head. "No champagne this trip, princess. Coffee and canned fruit will have to do."

"Spoilsport." She took advantage of her freedom to jump to her feet.

Brock stood and stretched again. "I'll put the coffee on if you want to . . ." his voice trailed off.

"To what?" she asked innocently.

He offered her a rakish grin. "Clean up for breakfast, of course."

Her broad smile met his. "Of course." She grabbed her overnight bag and headed to the stream.

The icy water numbed her fingers, but that didn't stop her from washing her face until it, too, was tingling. She considered washing her hair, but the water was too cold. Maybe later in the day when she and the air were both warm, Brock would find another stream and she could wash it then. But for now, she simply brushed it until the tangles were out, then smoothed it over the bruise as best she could.

She rocked back on her heels and tried to decide if she wanted to go to the trouble of applying some makeup. Her expensive brand of mascara hadn't smeared yet, and she finally made up her mind that that was sufficient. She hoped Brock preferred the fresh-scrubbed look. Even if he didn't, he'd probably give her a hard time if she came back with her face made up like a model.

The strong smell of coffee greeted her as she walked to the camp fire. "You know, that stuff smells better than it tastes," she told Brock as he poured thick black coffee into two cups.

"I watered it down a little this morning, just for you." He handed her a cup. "Hungry?"

"Famished," she admitted. The coffee didn't taste much different to her, and her stomach gurgled its protests as soon as she swallowed.

"Good. Here's your breakfast." He held out an open can of sliced peaches with a spoon stuck in it.

Jami cocked her head to one side and eyed the can. "Such exquisite dinnerware. Wherever did you get it?"

"Blue light special at Tiffany's. It's the disposable kind. Eat off it once and throw it away. It's the latest rage in Paris."

She took the can from him and stuck a tangy peach in her mouth. "It looks to me like you're trying to get out of doing the dishes."

"Ah, the lady has brains as well as beauty," he said playfully. "You weren't supposed to figure me out."

In minutes Jami had finished her small meal. "I'm going to go brush my teeth before we go," she announced while Brock was putting out the fire.

"I don't suppose you have two toothbrushes?" he asked rather wistfully.

"Sorry, I just brought one."

"You shared the blanket with me last night. How about your toothbrush?"

She wrinkled her nose at him. "You want to use my toothbrush?"

"Sure. You don't mind, do you?"

"Well," Jami said doubtfully. Sharing a toothbrush seemed almost more intimate than sharing a blanket. Still, she supposed it wasn't all that big a deal. "All right," she agreed at last.

"Thanks." He grabbed the toothbrush and toothpaste out of her hand. "I'll go first."

She watched him saunter off to the stream as if he owned the world. But then, she supposed he did own this world, the one they were in right here, right now. And she was definitely the visitor. But what would she be when she finally got to Hank's ranch?

She sighed deeply, remembering how good it had felt to be tucked in Brock's arms while they slept. Nor could she forget how he'd brought every sense in her body to sizzling awareness when he'd kissed her in the plane. Yet he could also make her so mad sometimes she could cheerfully strangle him. No, she'd never met a man who was so unpredictable or who could bring out such a wide variety of emotions in her. Nevertheless, the man was merely one of her grandfather's employees. She had to keep reminding herself of that.

Jami reached down and pulled Hank's letter out of her overnight case. She opened it up carefully and reread its brief contents for the twentieth time.

> Jamaica: My health is steadily declining, and it's time I faced reality. Soon I will no longer be able to run my ranch, and very soon after that, I will be gone entirely. I've thought a great deal about who to leave my ranch to, and you, my granddaughter, seem like the only reasonable candidate. I would appreciate it if you could come out to Montana as soon as possible so we can discuss this further.
>
> Hank

No matter how many times she read the letter, she couldn't help feeling surprised. What, after all, did she know about running a cattle and horse ranch? She had to admit the letter couldn't have come at a better time in her life, though. A few months ago, she would have dismissed the letter entirely and never ventured to the ranch. But the more she thought about it, the more her grandfather's letter intrigued her.

At the sound of cheerful whistling, Jami hastily folded the letter and stuffed it among her toiletries. She was becoming increasingly aware of one potential difficulty she would face if she did take over Hank's ranch.

She would be Brock's boss.

She had the uneasy feeling that he would never accept that. Actually, how many men on Hank's ranch would accept an inexperienced city woman being in charge? If she got involved with Brock out here, it would destroy their chances for having any kind of working relationship at the ranch.

She could just imagine him bragging to all the other cow-hands how he'd slept with the boss. Well, she would have to cross that bridge when she came to it. For now, she had to concentrate on getting to the ranch. And her chances of that depended on the man who was now walking up to her with a wide and appealing smile on his face.

Strong, tanned fingers held out her toothbrush and toothpaste. "They're all yours. I really appreciate your letting me use them."

"No problem." Jami took them from him, being careful not to touch his hand. She couldn't help feeling attracted to him, and even though he might not like her very much, she knew he was attracted to her. In their present surroundings, such a combination was volatile at best.

Considering that her future on Hank's ranch might depend on keeping things platonic with Brock, it would be wise not to invite any extra physical contact between them. The easiest way to do that was to remind herself over and over who he was and who she was.

As Jami strolled slowly down to the stream to brush her teeth, she realized the only trouble with that was, it was fast becoming less and less important.

Four

———

I know it was part of our deal that I don't complain," Jami called out to Brock as the distance between them gradually increased, "but I'm complaining now! I need a break!"

It was nearly one o'clock in the afternoon, and they'd been walking steadily since leaving the stream that morning. The canteen, which had been empty and nothing more than a nuisance the day before, was now filled with water and felt like a brick. Her shoulders ached with every step. Her tennis shoes, so comfortable in the health club, had started rubbing painfully against her feet several hours ago. Her stomach was rumbling, and she was dreadfully thirsty.

If only Brock would let her have a few sips out of the canteen, it would kill two birds with one stone: it would soothe her parched throat as well as lighten her load. But he'd firmly told her they couldn't drink until they stopped for lunch because he didn't know when he would find another creek.

Brock didn't even glance over his shoulder. "We've got to keep moving. You can make it a little farther."

Jami stopped. "No, I can't." She was sick and tired of his dictatorial attitude. Why couldn't he show a little compassion once in awhile? She'd done her best to keep up with him all day, and he'd only rewarded her with snarling commands to keep going.

She dropped her overnight bag to the ground and hitched the canteen off her shoulder. Feeling delightfully naughty, she unscrewed the cap and took a long drink of the cool water. She replaced the cap and sat down.

It was several minutes before Brock noticed the lack of sound from behind him. He turned and saw Jami sitting quite a way behind him, her arms crossed stubbornly over her chest.

"What do you think you're doing?" he yelled with more than a little impatience. He had no time for these games of hers.

"What does it look like I'm doing?" she shouted back. "I'm taking a break!"

"Have you taken a look at the sky lately?" he asked sardonically, motioning upward with one hand.

Jami followed the direction he was pointing and saw the sky was filled with dark gray swirling clouds. Come to think of it, she'd noticed the sun had disappeared about an hour ago, but she hadn't given it much consideration at the time. "So? It's cloudy. Big deal."

Brock shook his head in annoyance. "It's going to rain in less than an hour. If we don't get farther up this mountain before it hits, we're going to end up in the middle of a storm with no protection. Now get up and get moving." He turned around and started walking again.

She frowned and closed her eyes. Maybe, if she tried hard enough, she could wish herself already at her grandfather's ranch, sitting comfortably in the kitchen eating a big piece of apple pie complete with vanilla ice cream. And while she was at it, she would wish Brock far, far away where he couldn't boss her around and make her miserable.

She slowly opened her eyes. And sighed. It didn't work. She was still stuck out in the middle of nowhere with an unfeeling brute of a man who wasn't slowing down one bit to wait for her. Well, if she sat there long enough, half her wish would come true. Brock would be far away in no time.

The realization of that was enough to spur her into reluctant but hostile action. She dragged herself to her feet, picked up her two loads and started after him. The creep probably wouldn't even miss her if she didn't follow him, she thought irritably. And to think this morning she'd actually thought she liked him a little! That idea seemed outrageously funny. Why he was the most arrogant, insufferable, egotistical, rude—

"Brock!" The word squeezed itself out of her lungs before her feet went out from under her. One minute she was navigating a steep, rocky incline, the next her shoes had slipped and she felt like she was moving in slow motion as she fell backward and was suspended in midair for an eternity before landing flat on her back.

She lay there for what seemed like hours, struggling with every ounce of strength in her body to breathe. But she couldn't get any oxygen into her gasping lungs. Panic and terror threatened to overtake her completely, but then the gray sky was replaced by Brock's face. She reached out and desperately grabbed at his shirt, trying to pull herself up and speak at the same time. She wasn't successful in either endeavor, which only alarmed her all the more. Why couldn't she breathe? Why didn't Brock do something?

"Take it easy, Jami," she heard Brock say in a maddeningly calm voice. "Try to relax. Your breath will come back in a second."

She shook her head, tears in her eyes, trying to make him understand it wouldn't. And then she finally got one tiny bit of air into her burning lungs, and then another, and another. She gratefully took in the air like a drowning swimmer grabs a lifeline, and in several minutes her breathing, although still erratic, was almost normal enough for her to realize that death had spared her again.

"You really didn't have to go to such an extreme to get a little rest," Brock said dryly.

She glared at him until she noticed how white he was and how tension had tightened up his features. Could it be that he was concerned about her?

"There's nothing quite as scary as having the breath knocked out of you, is there?" Brock's voice was all at once gentle and sympathetic. "How's your back?"

"All right," she told him, but that was far from the truth. It hurt like the devil, but what was one more ache? At least it took her mind off her feet and shoulders and stomach.

"See if you can sit up. If you feel a lot of pain, say something right away. You may have damaged your back, and if so, you shouldn't move."

With one arm supporting her shoulders, Brock helped pull her into a sitting position. Her back throbbed dully, but there was no sharp pain.

"Okay?" he questioned her. Jami nodded. "What happened? I heard you yell and then I heard a thud."

"I slipped going up there." She pointed at the rocks in front of her.

"With tennis shoes on?"

Jami crossed one leg over the other so he could see the soles of her shoes. "These are aerobic tennis shoes. They're not made for the great outdoors. There's no traction."

"You're lucky you didn't break your neck," he growled.

"It's not my fault I didn't bring hiking boots in case I happened to be in a plane crash!" she snapped. "You're the one who insisted I wear these shoes instead of any of my boots, remember?"

"I just assumed they would have normal traction on them. I forgot rich city people own impractical shoes."

"These shoes are perfect for the purpose they were intended for. You'd look pretty foolish in a health club wearing those boots you have on now, but that doesn't mean they're impractical, does it?"

The image of him working out in his heavy boots was enough to make them both laugh. "You're right," Brock admitted at last. "I'm sorry I barked at you. I was worried about you being hurt, and I guess I overreacted."

"Apology accepted," she said quietly, meeting his warm sapphire eyes. A tiny shiver went through her, but she bit her lip to bring herself out of his spell. She'd decided she didn't like him before her fall, so why was her heart suddenly pounding? And why should a new ache start to form deep inside her?

Brock read the look in her eyes and felt a gnawing ache build in him, too. He wondered if she had any idea what she'd been putting him through since they had met. One minute he was cursing the fates that had brought them together and hoping he'd never see her again, then the next instant he couldn't get enough of just looking at her. Did she know how soft her hair was, how tasty her lips looked? And her body—her body was made for loving a man. Not just any man, he corrected himself, although he was sure there'd been a few in her life, but him. He'd already found out from sleeping next to her that she molded against him more perfectly than any other woman had in his life.

"Damn you," he muttered softly.

Jami's eyes widened in surprise. "What?"

Brock cleared his throat. "Let's go," he said gruffly, pulling her to her feet. Pondering about what lovely treasures were beneath her clothes was just plain stupid and very, very dangerous, and he knew it.

"Can't we rest for a little while longer?" Jami protested weakly. Brock's sudden about-face had left her dizzy. She had thought for a moment there he was going to kiss her, so intense was his gaze. Now he seemed indifferent and aloof again.

"You said you were all right, didn't you?"

"Well, yes, but—"

"The storm is still coming. We've got to get farther up the mountain." He bent and picked up the canteen. "I'll carry this for you until we stop. But you can carry your own damn makeup case."

"There's more than just makeup in there!" she corrected him defensively as she ordered her feet to start moving one in front of the other. She would never admit she was beginning to wonder if it was really necessary for her to bring along as many toiletries as she'd thought were so vital when they'd left the plane.

When Brock offered her his hand to help her get up the slick incline she'd fallen on minutes before, she took it despite how much it grated on her to do so. Still, she had no desire to end up on her back again, so she let him assist her until they were over the worst of the rocks. Then she pulled her small hand away from his large, callused one and trudged along behind him in silence.

Brock's prediction turned out to be correct. Forty-five minutes later, a few drops of rain began to splatter around them. At first, Jami welcomed the refreshing feeling of the cool rain on her face and scalp, but in no time the pleasure turned to discomfort as she became wet and chilled. Right before it started to pour, Brock located a small indentation in the side of the mountain where they could just, by sitting cross-legged, stay dry.

"It isn't much, but it's the best shelter I can find right now," Brock said. "If the rain had held off a bit longer, I'm sure I could have found some kind of cave a little farther up."

"Cave?" Jami repeated uneasily. "Don't caves have inhabitants? Like bears and snakes and bats?"

Brock smiled. "Sometimes."

"Really, this isn't so bad here," she said quickly. At least they didn't have to fight to be the only occupants. Besides, it felt heavenly to sit down, no matter where it was. "Is it time for lunch now?"

"Sure. The way the sky looks, we'll probably be here for supper, too." He opened up the blanket and took out several sticks of beef jerky.

Jami took two sticks of the dried beef from him. "This is it?"

"Of course not," Brock said cheerfully. He picked up the canteen. "You also get some water."

"Ah, such filling cuisine. I hope my stomach has room for this feast."

"Eat slow," he advised with a chuckle, then sobered. "Every minute it rains during the day means our food supply has to last that much longer. If it was the middle of the summer, I'd keep going despite the rain. But since it's only April, it's just too cold out there."

"And slippery," she added.

They ate without talking, and for a long time after they finished, they both stared out at the rain dripping down like a small waterfall over the top of their shelter. At a loud clap of thunder, Jami jumped and grabbed Brock's arm.

"Don't say it," she warned sternly.

"Say what?"

"You're not afraid of a simple thunderstorm, are you?" she recited mockingly.

Brock smiled and put his arm around her trembling shoulders. "I wasn't going to say that."

"Sure," she said accusingly. "Do you expect me to believe you'd let an opportunity pass without pouncing on my insecurities and irrational fears?"

Brock reached out and gently cupped her chin in his hand. Turning her face toward him, he stared intently into her green eyes that were crackling with challenge. "Jami?"

"What?" Her throat went dry, and she had difficulty swallowing. Her indignation dissolved into nothingness at the look he was giving her.

"Can I kiss you now?"

"What?"

"You told me in the plane never to kiss you again without your permission," he told her solemnly. "So now I'm asking. Can I kiss you?"

Brock didn't wait long for an answer. He lowered his head and claimed her lips in a hard, possessive kiss. At her instant response, he freely explored the warm recesses of her mouth with his tongue. When her tongue met his, he could only take it for a few seconds before he groaned and released her.

Her stomach felt like it had dropped to her toes. She'd thought the kiss they'd shared in the plane had been shattering. It was nothing compared to this one. "You didn't wait for me to say it was okay," she said breathlessly.

He smiled wryly. "You should feel honored I asked twice. I've never even asked a woman once before."

"I can believe that."

Brock turned to study her, his pulse working double time. "You should have said no," he told her softly.

"I know."

They sat in silence for a long time, listening to the drumming of the rain as it cadenced against the rock all around them. It was a soothing sound that helped extinguish the yearnings that had raged with such an intensity in them both only minutes before.

Vaguely Brock became aware that Jami was frequently shifting her position next to him. He glanced at her and caught the look of discomfort on her face before she could hide it.

"Is your back bothering you?"

Jami simultaneously raised her shoulders and arched her back. She winced at the dull ache the movement caused her. Sitting on the cold, hard ground was causing her back to stiffen up.

"A little," she admitted reluctantly.

Brock edged away from her and spread the blanket over the smooth rock. "Lie down on your stomach," he instructed.

She opened her mouth to protest, but the thought of lying prone was too tempting. She stretched her cramped body on the blanket, crossed her arms under her head and closed her eyes.

A moment later her eyes jerked open as she felt Brock's hands tentatively touching her back underneath her jacket.

"What—what are you doing?"

"Relax. I'm just going to massage your back." His hands became firm as he pressed on her tense muscles. "Tell me if I hit a spot that hurts too much."

Several times in the first few minutes of his massaging, Jami flinched but didn't stop him. After about ten minutes of steady, circular pressure from his fingers, she was able to relax completely. The pain had subsided, and she only felt wonderful pleasure from Brock's soothing hands.

"You missed your calling," she told him with a sigh. "You should've been a masseur instead of a cowhand."

"I'm a man of many talents," he said pointedly.

She felt his hands stray outward and stroke the sensitive area just to the sides of her rounded breasts. She gasped as her whole body started tingling, and she had no doubt Brock had spoken the truth. Then, abruptly, his hands were gone.

"I'm glad you're feeling better now." His voice had taken on a husky timbre that sent a shiver through her. "Why don't you rest here for awhile?"

As he started to leave their small shelter, Jami sat up in alarm. "Where are you going?"

"Outside."

"Why? It's still raining."

"I know. But not much." Seemingly as an afterthought, he bent to pick up the canteen. "I'm going to go see if I can find more water."

"Why don't you just stick your arm outside and let the canteen fill up with rain?"

He gave her a crooked smile. "Then I wouldn't get a cold shower at the same time, now would I?"

"Oh." She felt the color creep into her face. She pulled the blanket out from under her and curled up beneath it. She did feel a little tired, and she was plenty warm thanks to Brock's massage. "Well, be careful. And don't get lost."

"Me? Get lost?" he asked incredulously. "You've got to be kidding."

"Sorry to offend you. What I really meant was, don't lose me."

"Not a chance, princess," he said earnestly, his eyes raking over her wistfully. "Not a chance."

Five

When Jami awoke about an hour later, Brock hadn't returned. She felt momentarily worried, but quickly dismissed her worry as foolishness. Although a steady drizzle still fell, she decided to make the most of his absence by taking a quick trip to the bathroom. She stretched to test her back, which only ached a little, zipped her coat up and went out into the rain.

She was on her way back to the shelter when she heard Brock calling her. Loudly. She chose not to answer him right away, and continued on her way slowly. Let him worry about her for a change.

She was just about to the edge of the shelter when Brock came storming around from the other side.

"Where the hell were you?" he demanded angrily.

"Where do you think I was?" she countered smoothly. His hair was dripping wet, and his leather jacket was as shiny as black silk from being throughly soaked by the rain.

"Why didn't you answer me?"

She noticed the small pile of wood that had been dumped unceremoniously inside the shelter. "Oh, I guess I didn't hear you."

Brock grunted in disbelief. "Right."

"You're drenched. Are you going to make a fire?"

He threw her another irritated glance before bending to reorganize the wood. "Yeah. We'll probably be stuck in here the rest of the afternoon."

"Can I help?"

"Sure. Sit down and stay put. I don't want to have to go looking for you."

"Fine! Next time I have to go to the bathroom, I'll do it right here so you won't have to wonder where I am!" She sat as far away from him as their limited shelter would allow. "Why is it all right for you to go strolling around for an hour when I can't go outside for five minutes alone?"

"That's different."

"Why?"

"Because I know my way around. And I don't panic when I hear animal noises. And I don't have on slippery shoes. And I'm not helpless."

"Neither am I! I could get along just fine out here without you," she informed him icily.

"Sure you could, sweetheart."

"Don't call me that."

"Sweetheart?" he repeated, sounding surprised. "Believe me, I didn't mean it endearingly."

"Thank God for small favors." She brought her knees to her chest and wrapped her arms tightly around her legs. Was this the same man who'd so recently kissed her with such passion and had massaged her back with such tenderness? The same man whom she'd wanted to do so much more to her?

Brock took a deep breath and let it out slowly. He was being rough on her, and he knew it. Spending nearly an hour in the rain had done little to improve his disposition. He'd returned to the shelter once while she was still sleeping, and the sight of her had sent him hastily back outside.

He never, never should have weakened and kissed her.
And letting his hands explore a little too far on her back had
almost been his undoing. He smiled in derision as he realized the pleasure it would bring Jami to know how he was
suffering for it now. Maybe that was why he was being such
a jerk. He wanted to make her suffer because it was her fault
that he felt as tightly coiled up as a rattler ready to strike.

He paused in his efforts to start a fire long enough to
glance at her. Her damp hair had curled around her face,
and she looked like a wet, forlorn, lost little girl. His anger
and hostility gradually released their ferver. He wanted to
apologize to her, but the words got stuck in his throat and
choked him. He coughed, hoping to get her attention, but
when she continued to stare at the ground in front of her feet
and wouldn't look at him, he turned back to making the
fire.

"Have you ever been married?"

Brock almost jumped at her soft question. He lifted his
eyes from the match he had just lit to meet her emerald gaze.
"What?"

"You heard me."

"No. Ow!" he yelled, dropping the match that had
burned down to lick at his fingers. As he sucked on his
scorched flesh, he wondered if she'd purposely asked him
such a bizarre question right at that moment to achieve just
that result.

"I can see why."

"Oh, yeah?" Brock shook his hand then lit another
match. This time he concentrated on it instead of her face.
"For your information, I've never asked anyone."

"Why not? Afraid no one would have you?"

"No. Actually, I've never met a woman who didn't bore
me after a few months. I've never found someone I could
imagine spending the rest of my life with."

"What an ego," Jami said, rolling her eyes.

He flinched a little at her jeering tone. He hardly ever
admitted the truth to anyone, for just that reason. Even he
didn't care much for the way it sounded. The tiny flame he'd

been fanning started igniting the wood, so he let his eyes rest on her again.

"Want to know something else?" he asked quietly.

She shrugged in an effort to appear indifferent, but there was something about the look on his face that brought her to instant alertness. "What?"

"I don't think you would bore me if we spent a hundred years together."

All she could do was stare at him in astonishment for a long time. When she finally spoke, her voice was weary and strained. "You give me a headache."

"I do? Why?"

"You just do." She couldn't, wouldn't explain it to him. Did he know what emotional turmoil he was putting her through?

"So what about you?"

"What about me?"

"Tell me about your love life. Ever been married?"

She laughed without humor. "No."

"Almost?" Brock prodded curiously.

"Yes. Almost."

Satisfied with the progress of the fire, Brock sat near Jami, but far enough away so that he couldn't easily touch her. "Sounds like an interesting story. Tell me about it."

"Now?"

"Sure. We've got all day."

Jami sighed and closed her eyes. "His name was Jonathon. He was from a decent family, but not a rich one like mine. My parents liked him, but by no means encouraged our relationship. I suppose that's one reason I was attracted to him, because they didn't really approve. After just a few wonderful months together, we got engaged."

"Then what happened?" Brock urged when she was silent for a few minutes.

Jami frowned at the memory. "Jonathon started putting pressure on me to get my father to let him into his business once we got married. I guess I should have seen through him then, like my father did. Daddy told me he was just after the family money, but I couldn't believe that. I was so sure Jonathon loved me as much as I loved him. I shared every-thing in my life with him. Everything." Jami turned to look at Brock to emphasize the last word, making sure he under-stood her meaning.

He did. His chest tightened, and his right hand balled into a tense, angry fist. He wasn't sure he wanted to hear any more. He'd had no idea hearing about Jami with another man would affect him so much. "Go on," he said at last, his voice barely controlled.

"One lovely evening, I decided to surprise Jonathon at his apartment with some carryout Chinese food. I had a key because I was over there so much. I burst in, and the rest, as they say, is history."

"He was with another woman?"

She nodded. "He threw her out and spent the next half hour trying to convince me she didn't mean anything to him, that it was me he loved. Of course I couldn't believe that." She laughed again, a high-pitched, hollow laugh. "Do you know the worm actually tried to tell me being unfaithful was no big deal, that once we were married, he wouldn't care if I slept around, too? He made me sound like a prude be-cause I didn't believe in having an open marriage."

"So you dumped him," Brock finished for her.

"Yes." She glared pointedly at Brock. "And I made up my mind that day not to get involved with another man who was poor, because I could never be sure he wasn't after my money. Jonathon was a hell of an actor, but I'm sure there are a lot of others who are even more convincing."

Brock shifted uncomfortably. "Meaning me?"

"Maybe."

Tell her the truth, a tiny voice inside him ordered. *Tell her you've got lots of your own money, so she knows you're not after hers.* But he couldn't. How in the world could he tell her he owned the ranch adjoining Hank's place? That he had nearly twice the land and cattle her grandfather had? His wealth didn't come close to Jason McKenzie's, but with all his investments, he was one of the richest ranchers in Montana.

He opened his mouth, but the words wouldn't come out. He'd sound like a fool telling her now, after all this time. Especially if he told her after the story about her fortune-seeking boyfriend. Oh, he knew she'd find out as soon as they got to Hank's, and he hoped she would be so embarrassed she'd turn tail and run to New York where she belonged. That, after all, was what he wanted, wasn't it? He'd do just about anything to keep her from getting Hank's ranch, wouldn't he? Wasn't that what really mattered to him?

Suddenly he wasn't sure anymore. Somewhere along the line, all his clear-cut thinking had become muddled. He was beginning to wonder what her reaction would be when she found out who he was. He had the feeling she'd be more spiteful than anything else.

Brock grabbed her arm in frustration. Then let it go when she flinched. "I'm not like Jonathon." *But you're just as deceitful,* the tiny voice nagged. He ignored it as best he could.

"Tell me something, Brock. What happens to us when we get to my grandfather's ranch?"

"I guess that depends on you."

"Me? Why me?"

His smile held a touch of bitterness, and something that resembled regret. "I won't be any different when we get there. What you see out here is what you'll get at Hank's ranch. Sure, there are some things you don't know about me, but all in all, my personality won't change. However, I doubt I can say the same about you."

"I won't change, either," she told him firmly.

"Like hell, you won't. You've let your high-and-mighty attitude drop for the most part out here because I won't put up with it and you need me. But when we get to Hank's? You'll be the woman I met at the airport."

"I might surprise you."

"You might." He realized he actually hoped she would, but he couldn't count on it.

"And maybe you'll surprise me, too."

"In what way?"

"Maybe you wouldn't rush to tell all the other hands the first chance you got about the conquest you made on the boss's granddaughter." *Who is also their future boss,* she added silently.

"Assuming there was a conquest."

She shrugged. "Even if there wasn't."

"My affairs are my business," he said flatly. "No one else's. And I certainly wouldn't go to the trouble of making anything up."

"Oh, come on. Men are worse gossips than women."

"Not this man."

Jami was far from convinced. But when her stomach growled loudly a moment later, they both smiled, and the tension that had arisen between them drifted away. It was also a reminder of how late it was getting, and a good way to change the subject.

"Is it time for supper yet?" Jami asked brightly.

"Not really," Brock said after a moment, silently agreeing it was best to forget their conversation. After all, what good would talking about it do? "But I guess we can splurge." He fished a can of pork and beans out of the pile of supplies and set it in the middle of the small fire.

Jami stared glumly at the can. "I always thought it was just a fallacy that people in the West lived on pork and beans. Why couldn't Hank have stocked his plane with tastier emergency provisions?"

"There's lots of nutrition in that can. And the popularity of beans in the West is no fallacy. On cattle drives, we eat them every night."

"But I bet you have more than just beans."

"We do. Juicy steaks, this thick." He measured a three-inch spread between his thumb and forefinger.

"Stop it, please," Jami protested, her mouth instantly watering. "I can't take it."

Brock laughed. "Don't worry, princess. A couple more days and we'll get to Hank's, and you can eat all you want. But don't expect caviar. Hank doesn't have any of that around."

She wrinkled up her nose. "I hate caviar."

"Really? There might be hope for you yet."

She let that comment pass with only a mild glare. "Don't we get any of your special gourmet coffee tonight?"

"Nope. I didn't find any streams this afternoon, so we have to conserve water."

She didn't know whether to be disappointed or relieved. Although she was getting used to Brock's coffee, she knew it was one thing she wouldn't miss when they got to the ranch. Then she was brought up short as she realized what followed that thought. What *would* she miss that she had here?

The only thing she could readily think of was the camaraderie she shared with Brock. When they got to Hank's, that would be gone for good. She would be the boss, and he would be resentful. They would be rich girl and hired hand, instead of just a man and a woman. And if by some miracle Brock was nice to her, she wouldn't be able to deny the suspicion that it was only because of her money. No matter how he might pretend to the contrary, she knew she'd never be sure.

"Hurry up and eat," Brock said, interrupting her thoughts as she toyed with her beans.

"Why?" she asked, startled.

"Look outside. It's stopped raining."

"Does that mean we're going to start walking again today? We just got dry and warm from the fire. And it's so late."

"We've got a couple hours of light left. You don't want to waste them, do you? I thought you were the one in such a hurry to get to your grandfather's ranch."

"I am." At least, she thought she was. No, of course she was. She had to forget any fanciful ideas about Brock, and forget them quick. So what if he made her feel things that even Jonathon never had? But she was scared—scared that she would never again experience the delicious sensations Brock brought out in her. She knew with absolute clarity that if she didn't act while they were out here alone, the opportunity would be lost forever. She didn't want to spend the rest of her life wondering what it might have been like to be with him, yearning for something she'd never had and never would.

"I'll pack up the blanket so you can tend to the fire," she offered with a sigh. "Then we can get going."

Within minutes, they were once more on their way to a destination both had mixed feelings about reaching.

"We'll stop here for the night." Brock dropped the blanket pack and canteen to the ground in the middle of a small group of pine trees.

"Thank you, kind sir," Jami muttered, dropping her overnight case. She sat down and immediately untied her shoelaces.

"What are you doing?"

She sighed in ecstasy as soon as the pressure was off her throbbing feet. It was nearly dark, and for the past hour she'd stubbed her already tender toes more times than she could count as she tried to keep up with Brock in the fading light. "Dying and going to heaven," she replied, then groaned. "How these feet are going to walk all day tomorrow in these shoes is totally beyond me."

Brock broke off an armful of dead branches from the pines around them. "After I get a fire going, we'll take a look at those feet. If they're as bad as you say, they might need some doctoring."

"You mean we might get to use the first-aid kit that's been breaking my shoulder for two days?"

"It's not the first-aid stuff that's making that case heavy, and you know it."

"I might have to do without almost every modern convenience known to man out here, but there are some things I refuse to give up."

"Like nail polish and perfume?"

She cocked her head and narrowed her eyes. "Give me a little credit, please. I'm not quite that—"

"Vain?" he supplied.

"Stupid," she finished. She opened the case and pulled out a travel-size bottle of shampoo. She held it up for his inspection. "For example, if you ever find a stream again, this little item will be worth its weight in gold." She fished out her favorite scented bar of soap. "So will this. And if you're very, very nice to me, maybe I'll even share some with you."

Brock snorted. "Great. We'll get rescued, and I'll smell prettier than you."

Her grin was slowly replaced by a pensive frown. "I hate the thought of everyone worrying about us. I wonder what Hank told my parents."

"Hank doesn't talk to your father much as a rule, does he?" Brock knew there was some deep feud between the two men, but Hank had never explained what the problem was.

"That's an understatement. I don't think they've spoken once in the past ten years." Jami pulled off her wet shoes and placed them close to the fire Brock had started. She tentatively massaged her aching feet.

"Your father must not have been very happy about you coming out here."

"He hated the idea."

"But you went against his wishes."

She nodded. "Maybe that's why I've stayed away from the ranch for so long. Hank and I have kept in touch with brief letters over the years, but whenever I even mentioned visiting him, my father had a fit."

"So why did you come now?"

"Hank needed me, and I needed to come," she said simply. "Has his health really been poor lately?"

"It hasn't been good. He doesn't even go down to the barns much anymore. He spends most of his time in the house, and for Hank, that's like a living hell."

Jami remembered how active and vital a man Hank had been that summer she'd spent with him, and it was torture to think of him as a near invalid. Brock was right; losing his mobility would be enough to kill him.

"And now he probably thinks I'm dead," she whispered. Anguish mixed with guilt as she realized how little she'd thought of her grandfather and what he must be going through since the crash. She'd been so preoccupied with Brock, she'd forgotten the rest of the people in her life.

"He's probably not even worried." Brock's voice was husky with emotion. "He knows I'm the best pilot around, and he knows I'll take good care of you. He wouldn't send just anyone to get you, you know."

She smiled hopefully and struggled to hold back the tears that had dampened her eyes. "Did he talk about me very much? I mean, was he glad I was coming?"

"He seemed quite relieved you were coming," he told her carefully. "And he has told me stories about how his sprite of a granddaughter could practically outride all his cowhands when she was hardly out of diapers."

"He was exaggerating," she said, laughing. "I was twelve." Crusty old Hank, proud of her? It felt good to hear it, no matter how unlikely it seemed.

"He's a wonderful old man. Hard to get to know, but special once you do," Brock said softly. He squatted in front of Jami. "Take off your socks. I want to have a look at those feet."

Jami hastily tucked her legs underneath her. She didn't want Brock anywhere near her feet. "They're fine, really," she assured him.

"Let me see them," Brock said impatiently.

"No."

"Jami—"

"No!"

"Do you want them to get infected? Or how about having them amputated? If, that is, you can make it to Hank's ranch at all."

Iron wills clashed as they glared hotly at each other. Finally, Jami moved so both feet were in front of her and crossed her arms over her chest. "There! Look at them to your heart's content."

Brock bit on his lower lip to keep from smiling. He bent beside her, and in one quick, easy motion stripped off her left sock. "Damn."

At the back of her heel and on the side of her little toe were popped blisters. Her big toe sported a dark blue bruise under the nail. "I don't suppose the other foot is any better?" he said, more to himself than to her.

Jami didn't comment as he peeled off her other sock with much greater care. She was relieved to see her right foot only had one blister. "At least you know I had a reason to complain."

"Yeah," he said grudgingly. "Get the first-aid supplies out of your bag."

Jami did as she was told. After warning her it might sting, Brock sparingly poured peroxide over all the blisters. She watched in fascination as the clear liquid bubbled up into white foam. It did sting, more than a little, but she clamped her mouth shut so she wouldn't utter a sound. Brock let the peroxide dry before dabbing antiseptic ointment on the blisters, then he covered them all with bandages.

"Why don't you put on clean socks," he suggested as he stood and straightened his back. He was rather proud of himself for tending to her in a strictly clinical, detached manner. He'd been severely tempted to rub her tired feet and massage her calves, then maybe rub just a little farther up, but he'd kept his urges tightly under control. All his urges. And it hadn't been easy.

"All right." She dug through her case until she located her other pair of socks. "And thanks for patching my feet up."

"No problem."

She watched Brock as he awkwardly tidied up the first-aid supplies. "I think I'll turn in, if you don't mind," she said after a moment. She didn't know what else to say or do, so going to bed seemed like the only alternative.

"Sure, go ahead." He handed her the blanket. "I want to get an early start tomorrow. We'll go a little slower with your feet being the way they are."

She nodded thankfully. "Well, good night."

"Good night."

Jami turned away from him and rolled her body into a fetal position under the blanket. She closed her eyes. Unwilling memories of Brock's strong body next to her drifted into her mind instantly. She opened her eyes and sighed quietly. She wanted Brock to sleep beside her again, but the mood wasn't right to ask him. Last night it had simply slipped out while she was in a stupor of exhaustion and stress. But tonight, if she asked him, it would seem like she was really asking him to do more than just sleep.

She closed her eyes again, ordering herself to relax. But it was two restless hours before her body gave up on what it really wanted and she dropped off into a deep sleep.

She was dreaming. She and Brock were in the plane, spinning at a crazy speed toward the side of a cliff. She screamed and screamed until her lungs burned as the cliff got closer and closer....

She awoke with a start, her eyes wide and her body trembling. It took her a few minutes to get her bearings and realize it had been a nightmare. If only it hadn't been so vivid, so horrifying.

"You all right?"

She nearly jumped out of her skin. Brock was lying with his back to her and hadn't moved, so she'd thought he was still asleep.

"Yes," she whispered, but her voice was unsteady.

"Bad dream?"

"You could say that."

"Do you want to talk about it?" The words were ripped reluctantly from him before he could stop them. He hadn't wanted to ask, hadn't wanted to get too close, too involved.

"It was just about the plane crash." She simultaneously sniffed and shuddered. She was starting a new life, but she'd been perilously close to losing everything before she'd had the chance to begin again. The nightmare was an unwelcome reminder of that, and of just how much more she had to lose only two days later.

The tears fell finally, silently, or so she thought until all at once Brock was beside her, pulling her into his arms. She pressed her face against his chest and wept away her fear of starting over and her fear of the feelings she was developing for the man who was holding her.

Determination and optimism gradually replaced uncertainty and anxiety, causing the tears to abate at last. She lifted her head from Brock's soggy T-shirt. On an impulse, she kissed him lightly on his bristly cheek. "Thanks for the shoulder."

"Any time." His skin tingled where her warm lips had caressed his face. It was all he could do not to bring his hand up to his cheek to either rub the kiss in or rub it out. He couldn't make up his mind which he felt more like doing.

"And Brock?" The small distance between them had become charged with passionate electricity, but she didn't regret the brief kiss. What she really needed just then, however, was a little levity.

"Yes?" His eyes roamed over her face, pausing to rest hungrily on her lips.

"You desperately need a shave."

It took a moment for her words to sink in, but when they did, he burst out into hearty laughter. By now he should expect the unexpected from her, he told himself. But her flippant remark gave him an excuse to run his fingers over his cheek, and when he did, he decided he was rubbing her kiss into his prickly, half-bearded face.

"You're right," he said ruefully. "I don't suppose you have a razor in that handy bag of yours, do you?"

"What? You're asking to borrow one of my personal belongings that you've been harassing me for two days for carrying?" she teased in mock disbelief. "Not on your life, buster."

"Come on, Jami."

"Besides," she added thoughtfully, cocking her head to one side to study his profile in the dim firelight, "you look kind of dashing in a beard."

"That may be, but in another day or two it's going to itch like hell."

"Well, ask me again when it does. And I'll think about it."

His heated gaze rested on her face for a long time as he battled with himself to keep from kissing her. Really kissing her.

"You'd better try to get some more sleep," he finally murmured. He turned away from her. "It's almost morning."

She could only stare at him. The veiled curtain had slipped over his features again, putting an unbridgeable gap between them. Well, two could play at that game. She didn't answer as she laid down and covered herself up to her nose with the blanket. She doubted sleep would claim her whirling mind, but she could fake it with the best of them.

Brock watched her out of the corner of his eye, knowing by her stiff posture that she was angry at his dismissal and certainly not asleep. He grabbed a long stick of wood and poked irritably at the fire. He didn't want to care about her. He didn't want to share so many pleasant times with her. It would be pure emotional suicide to get involved with Jamaica McKenzie. But damn it, he was already involved. His wanting her went far beyond the physical ache he had to make love to her. And it grated on him terribly to admit it to himself.

He jabbed fiercely at the fire again, sending shooting sparks in every direction as the wood resettled. His eyes flitted from one spark to another but they burned out almost as soon as they landed. All except one. One troublesome spark had fallen on Jami's blanket, and in moments it brightened and grew.

He ran over and jerked the blanket away from her body in one swift movement. He heard her let out a surprised yelp just before he beat the blanket against the ground, extinguishing the single tiny flame. Only then did he look at her. She'd jumped instinctively to her feet, her large green eyes wide and startled.

Jami swallowed the fear that had sent her heart racing as the reasoning behind Brock's seemingly erratic behavior became clear. "That was certainly a rude awakening," she commented dryly.

"Like hell. You weren't asleep."

"How do you know?" Her pulse quickened as he stepped near her. He handed her the blanket. She took it from him, but her gaze was locked squarely on his face.

"You weren't snoring."

She threw him an exasperated look. "I never snore."

"Are you sure about that?"

"Absolutely," she said, hoping she was right. "Anyway, I'm glad you were awake when the fire popped like that. You saved me from what could've been a nasty burn."

He shrugged. "I'm the one who made the fire spark to begin with."

"Why weren't you trying to sleep? The fire was burning fine."

"Sleep? How could I sleep when all I could think about was kissing you?" he ground out.

The blanket dropped from her hands. She reached up and entwined her fingers behind his neck, bringing her face to within inches of his. "That's why I couldn't sleep, either," she whispered breathlessly.

With a stifled groan, Brock closed the distance between their lips. It was a wild and urgent kiss that barely expressed the explosive passion they both felt. Her inviting mouth opened to allow his hot tongue an eager and thorough exploration of its softness. A moment later, when her tongue met his, they both moaned in sweet agony.

Brock lowered them to the ground and covered the length of her with his tightly muscled body. Hardly aware that he did so, he pressed demandingly against the cradle of her thighs.

His fingers slipped beneath her sweater and caressed their way up to one of her taut breasts. Her aroused nipple met his palm with only the thin fabric of her bra separating them. Jami inhaled sharply, and her breast pressed more firmly against his hand.

"God, how I want you," he muttered, his lips roaming from her mouth to her chin to her neck.

Her whole body was throbbing with such intensity that she could hardly hear him. She was lost in the flood of exquisite sensations Brock was making her feel, sensations that she'd never before felt with such urgency. She couldn't get close enough to him, and she desperately wished their clothing wasn't in the way. Just then Brock started to pull off her jacket, and she realized she was about to get her wish.

The reality of that was paralyzing. She froze.

She wasn't ready for this. She'd thought she was, but doubts came tumbling forward. They had too far left to travel to be intimate yet. She couldn't be sure of how Brock would treat her in the morning; in fact, she couldn't be sure he wouldn't scorn her once he got what he wanted. She couldn't take that chance.

Brock felt her tense and backed off immediately. He ached so much for her it was painful, but he wouldn't push.

"I'm sorry, Brock," Jami said quietly. Brock was still so close to her he was like a second skin, but his hands and mouth had stopped their passionate perusal. How had he known almost before she had that she couldn't go through with it?

"Yeah." He grunted and eased his hips away from her. The sooner he got some space between that area of their bodies the better.

She missed the contact immediately. It took a big surge of willpower to keep from arching against him. "I just don't think it's a good idea," she said, more unsteadily than she wanted to.

"Because I'm just a cowhand?"

She looked at him in amazement. "No. Believe it or not, that thought hadn't entered my mind." And she knew she was speaking the truth. That was the part that stunned her.

"Believe it or not, I believe you." He tried to pass off the exhilaration her words gave him, but he couldn't. What was happening to him? What kind of spell had this woman cast?

He released his hold on her and pushed himself stiffly to his feet. Then he offered her his hand. She took it, and he pulled her up. They took a couple of steps away from the fire, both so feverish they no longer needed the heat from the flames.

Brock smiled at her lovely, flushed face. "Look at the sky," he said in a voice that was still throaty with desire.

Frowning, she saw that the horizon had lightened to reveal colorful shades of crimson and pink. "It's morning already?"

"I'm afraid so. How about some breakfast?"

How about finishing what we started, her body screamed silently. Instead, she sighed. "Sure."

When she reached out to take a can of pears from him, Brock caught her outstretched fingers with his free hand and pressed a kiss into her palm. "Until next time, princess."

An involuntary shiver ran through her as she ran her tongue over lips that were chafed and a little raw. "Brock?"

"Hmm?"

"Remind me to let you use my razor before then."

By the time the sun rose a few minutes later, the new day had already been warmed by their shared laughter.

Six

Jami was following closely behind a slowly moving Brock, concentrating on strategically placing her feet where her toes wouldn't get stubbed, when her forehead ran into the solid wall of his back. Brock stumbled forward from the impact, then turned and grasped her shoulder.

"Keep your chin up, princess," he said cheerfully. "Look down there."

She followed the direction of his outstretched hand and saw paradise about half a mile below them. "A stream!" She clapped her hands together in excitement.

"That's not just a stream. It's a river. And not only will we have water to drink and bathe in, I know right where this river is in relation to Hank's ranch."

For the moment, she was more thrilled about drinking freely and washing her hair and body than she was about getting closer to the ranch. Brock took her hand, and they ran down the hillside together, through scattered wild-flowers and scrub trees, laughing like a couple of kids, her sore feet forgotten. They reached the bank of the river out of breath and collapsed several feet from the water.

"This is so wonderful," Jami managed to get out, still gulping air while her heart slowed to a normal pace. "Do you think the water's freezing cold?"

"Who cares? It's wet, and that's all that matters." Then his attention was drawn to the water by a splashing sound not far away from where they sat. He leaped to his feet to investigate. Seconds later he let out a loud whooping yell that echoed in the hills around them.

"What is it?" Her eyes widened in shock and delight as Brock scooped a huge, squirming fish out of the river.

"This, my dear, is lunch. Real, fresh fish, slowly roasted over an open fire. It'll almost be better than steak," he promised with a huge grin.

"I can't believe it!" She ran to his side to examine the pink and brown fish. "What kind is it?"

"Trout."

"However did you catch it? I thought only Indians could just reach in and pull fish out of the water."

Brock laughed at the amazed expression on her face. He almost didn't want to tell her, she was looking at him with such admiration and respect. "See that little pool right there?" He pointed to a spot at the side of the river in front of them. "See how there are rocks all around it? This big fella must've jumped in there, then was trapped. It was easy to grab him. He had nowhere to go."

"But why didn't he just jump out again?"

"Fish aren't that smart, Jami. He got in there by accident and couldn't figure out how to get out."

She flashed him a sweet smile. "Well, while you fix up this delicious feast, I'm going to go downriver and freshen up for lunch."

"Don't you want to help me clean him?" he teased. At the look of horror on her face, he chuckled. "Go on, get out of here. But don't go too far. Stay within earshot and holler if you need me."

"You'll stay right here until I get back?" she asked suspiciously as she picked up her overnight case.

"Scout's honor." He gave her a lewd wink. "Don't take too long, though. I might get worried and have to come looking for you. Quietly."

"I'll remember that when it's your turn to bathe," she tossed over her shoulder as she swept past him.

"I wouldn't mind," he called.

No, he probably wouldn't, she decided as she wound her way down the river until she was satisfied she was out of his sight but not out of hearing. Jami felt filthier than she ever had in her life. She carefully removed her treasured bottle of shampoo and bar of soap, along with her clean clothes—jeans, panties and pullover shirt. She laid them out on a rock at the river's edge. Then she hastily stripped off her clothes and tiptoed into the water.

It was cold, but not as cold as she'd expected. Although her body was instantly covered with goose bumps, once she slipped underneath the surface of the deepest part of the river, she felt luxuriously invigorated. For several minutes, she swam around, enjoying the feeling of freedom as the water gently washed away three days worth of sweat and grime.

After she'd thoroughly scrubbed her hair and body, she climbed almost reluctantly onto the shore. She squeezed the excess drips out of her hair and stood with her face pointed toward the midday sun while the warm rays dried her body.

Once she was dressed, she combed all the tangles out of her hair and then studied her face in her compact. All her mascara had worn off, so she applied a touch to accent her green eyes. Her wet, curly bangs barely covered the bruise on her forehead, and she hoped her hair would be dry enough to conceal it by the time Brock saw her.

Jami picked up her overnight case to take with her, but she left her shampoo, soap, comb and a razor on the rock for Brock to use. As she walked, the pleasant odor of roasting fish drifted to her, making her stomach growl and her mouth water in anticipation. She rounded the last bend in the river to see Brock kneeling by a crackling fire. Several large fillets were speared on a stick over the flames.

Brock looked up and smiled as she approached. "You look great," he said simply. His eyes skimmed every inch of her before coming to rest on her face.

"And that fish smells great. How long before we eat?"

Brock stood and stretched. "Just long enough from now for me to clean up. Looking at you makes me feel incredibly grimy." He paused and got a sheepish grin on his face. "Okay, I'm going to eat crow now and ask you for that shampoo and soap."

She laughed and patted his rough cheek. "Go around three bends in the river, and you'll find everything you need. Even my razor."

"You're an angel. I'll be back in a few minutes. Keep your eyes open for lunch guests."

"What do you mean by that?" she yelled in alarm at his jogging back, but he only waved and kept on going. Frowning, she sat with her back close to the fire so her hair would finish drying. She didn't have much time to dwell on Brock's warning about wild animals dropping in, though, because in no more than ten minutes she heard him returning from the river.

The welcoming smile on her face faded into awe as he rounded the last corner and walked nonchalantly to the fire. All he was wearing was his jeans. His T-shirt, socks, and briefs were slung over his arm, leaving a dripping trail behind him. He hadn't bothered to wait for the sun to dry his skin, and tiny beads of water glistened on his bare, sinewy chest like diamonds scattered over gold. His face was clean-shaven again, and she decided he was much more handsome without a beard hiding his chiseled features. She watched him spread his clothes around the fire before she found her voice again.

"What are you doing?" Her eyes were riveted on the protruding muscles that flexed along his back and arms with every movement.

He paused to look at her with one eyebrow raised. He wondered if she had any idea how it affected him to see her so obviously appreciating his body. "I didn't come to pick you up at the airport with a suitcase full of clothes," he pointed out. "As you probably noticed, I've been wearing the same clothes for three days now. I thought it was about time they got washed, especially once I was clean."

"What about your jeans?" she said without thinking.

"I didn't want to shock you too badly," he said, amused at her discomfort. "But they do need washing, so since you don't mind. . . ." His hands moved to his belt buckle.

"No!" she objected immediately, then felt her face turn crimson. "I mean, uh, they don't look very dirty, really. Besides, denim takes forever to dry."

He sighed dramatically. "I suppose you're right. I guess I'll just have to put up with them the way they are." He chuckled at her undisguised look of relief and poked at the fish. "It's done. I hope you're good and hungry."

"You know I am," she assured him. She eagerly took the metal plate he offered her and tore into the meal with relish. The fish was so tender it broke into pieces beneath her fork. "Oh, Brock this is superb. This has to be the best-tasting food in the world."

"I have to agree with you. It does hit the spot, doesn't it?"

Jami only nodded, her mouth too full to answer. They ate the rest of their meal in silence, each intent on savoring the delicacy they'd been so lucky to find.

When Jami was finally so full that she was getting uncomfortable, she dropped her plate to the grass and lay on her back, her legs bent at the knees. As soon as her mind was off food, it turned to Brock's wonderful physique. She shut her eyes against the sight that created such turmoil within her own burning body.

"All done?" Brock asked.

"Yes. I don't think I'll have to eat another thing until tomorrow."

"The only trouble with eating something this good is that it's going to make our other food seem awfully bland."

Jami sat up and smiled. "I've got a news flash for you. That food we've been eating doesn't need anything to help it seem bland. It tastes that way all by itself."

"Maybe. But it's been better than starving, princess." Brock picked up his T-shirt and shook it out. "I guess my clothes are dry. I suppose I should get dressed again." He pulled the shirt over his head, undid his belt buckle and popped open the snap on his jeans. He paused to gaze thoughtfully at her.

Jami hastily got to her feet and scooped up their plates and forks. "I'll go do the dishes while you get dressed."

"Are you sure?"

"About what?" she challenged.

"That you want to wash the dishes. I could do them in a little while."

"What would I do instead?" she asked innocently.

"Watch."

"Really, Brock," she said a voice filled with as much boredom as she could muster. "Do you think I would see anything that I hadn't seen before?" She turned to hide her flushed face and walked to the river.

It only took a few minutes of swishing in the cool water to clean their dishes. A glance over her shoulder proved Brock was completely dressed and packing up their supplies. A smile lit up her face as she returned.

"Did you get everything back on where it belonged?" she asked teasingly.

"Yeah. Want to see for yourself?"

"No, no, that won't be necessary. I'll take your word for it. Here."

He took the dishes from her, his eyes never leaving her glowing face. She looked radiantly happy. He was feeling great, now that he was clean and had a full stomach, but he didn't expect her to be so—well, content with simple pleasures.

Jami shifted nervously beneath his scrutiny. "Stop looking at me like that."

"Like what?"

"Like you think I've finally lost all my marbles."

"Well," he said, scratching his head, "have you?"

She punched his arm and glared at him. "Of course not. What makes you think that?"

"You look like you haven't got a care in the world. Considering your situation, I just thought that was a little odd."

She sighed in exasperation. "Can't a girl simply be happy to be alive without some stupid man thinking she's crazy?"

"Stupid?" Brock repeated with mock severity.

"Yes, stupid. You're stupid if you think I'm crazy."

He snatched her arm and jerked her against his chest. "I don't think you're crazy. I think you're damn tough and not too bad looking, either."

"Gee, thanks," she said, acting put out even though her heart was pounding. "I'd rather be not too tough and damn good-looking."

He smiled warmly. "I stand corrected. You're damn tough and damn good-looking."

"Thank you." Her voice was husky, and she unconsciously wet her lips with her tongue.

The movement was not lost on Brock. He gazed hungrily at her perfectly shaped mouth for a moment before dragging himself away from her. "Come on. Let's get out of here before we end up wasting the rest of the afternoon on our backs."

"You think it would be a waste of the afternoon?" she said brazenly, and was instantly shocked. She'd never talked like that to any man. But when she saw his smoldering eyes burn even more intently into hers, she wasn't sorry for her impulsive words.

"No, princess. It wouldn't be a waste. But the nights are long out here, and they're much better suited for romantic interludes."

"Not to mention that our food supply is almost gone," she finished for him. "We can't afford to waste any time, right?"

"Right. If we hadn't lucked onto that fish, we'd be pretty bad off right now." He hitched the makeshift backpack over his shoulders and picked up the full canteen. His gaze lingered on her overnight case. "Is that thing really necessary? You'd do so much better without it."

"How can you say that when you had the privilege of enjoying half of what was in here such a short time ago?" she demanded.

"Half?" he scoffed. "I'd bet a thousand dollars that shampoo, soap, a comb and a razor do not make up half of what's in that case."

"Don't forget about the first-aid supplies."

"With so much of our canned food gone, I could easily fit the first-aid kit and those few other things in the blanket. But I refuse to carry all that other female garbage you have in there."

"Brock, we've had this conversation many times already. I'm doing just fine carrying this myself. And I'm going to keep on carrying it until we get to the ranch."

He shook his head. "Stubborn to the end, aren't you?"

She smiled sweetly. "No, just a woman to the end."

"You just elaborated on what I said. You didn't refute it."

She stuck her tongue out at him, but he was already on his way so he didn't notice.

"You know, when you say things like that, it sounds like you went to college. Did you?" she asked as she fell in step behind him. The realization hit her that she knew very little about this man.

He shrugged under the backpack. "Just because I don't drawl a lot of slang like your preconceived notion of a cowboy doesn't mean I'm highly educated."

"Was that a yes or a no?"

"Actually, I did go to college, but that's not the point."

"Where did you go?"

"The University of Montana. Are you impressed?"

She ignored his attempts to bait her. Now she knew why she didn't know much about him. He didn't exactly invite lengthy discussions about himself. But she wasn't about to give up. "What did you study?"

"Herd management, cattle breeding, the usual stuff."

"Are your parents still alive?"

"No."

"Do you have any brothers and sisters?"

Brock stopped suddenly and turned to face her. "Look, my past is far from interesting. I've never been one to wallow in my failures or brood over things I've never had. I live for today and I work for the future. Period. End of story."

"Fine!" she said fiercely, and swept past him.

His stomach rolled over at the hurt look so evident on her face. When he reached out to stop her, she flung his arm aside and kept walking. "Jami, hold on."

"Why? Aren't we in a big hurry to get to my grandfather's ranch? I know I am. The sooner I can get away from you, the better."

"Jami!" he barked, and she stopped. "You don't mean that," he said softly.

She whirled to face him, and he was surprised at the bitter intensity in her flashing eyes. "Maybe I do! Maybe I want to get there before I do something I'll regret!"

"I'd make sure you wouldn't regret it."

Her eyes narrowed as anger slipped away to be replaced by an uncontrollable swirl of longing. "You're impossible, do you know that?"

"So I've been told." He reached out to cup her chin with his hand. "I'm sorry. I didn't mean to upset you. I just don't like talking about myself. Besides, there are things about me that you're better off not knowing—for now, anyway."

She groaned. "That is a terrible thing to say. You know what curiosity did to the cat."

"I guess I'm glad you're not a cat," he said before his mouth covered hers. He'd been fighting the inevitable too long, and his strong resolve turned into undeniable desire.

His lips moved over hers tenderly as he invited her eager response. Surging need met surging need as their tongues touched, teased and entwined. The kiss shifted almost imperceptibly from a gentle expression of attraction and excitement to a wild depiction of deep yearning. Jami clung to Brock, afraid and unwilling to let go. She was astounded at how profoundly he affected her. Brock ignited a fire in her body that only he could extinguish, and nothing else mattered.

"I suppose I know all the important things about you," she conceded a moment later.

"Yes, you do. And you know more about me than you think. Thousands of people went to the same college I did. The simple fact that I went there doesn't tell you anything about the kind of man I am. You can only find that out for yourself, and not by asking a bunch of questions."

"I hate it when you say something that makes so much sense," she murmured.

He smiled and took her hand. "Come on, princess. We've got to make tracks while it's still light out."

When they finally stopped, it was dark. Dusk had settled in just as they'd reached a huge open valley, but they had kept going until they'd reached the safety of the treeline again. A tiny sliver of moon had helped guide them, but Jami was jumpy traveling in the dark with all the animal sounds that came to life when the sun went down. She couldn't see much of what she heard rustling around, but that was somehow worse.

It wasn't until Brock had a roaring fire built that she was able to relax. She took a deep breath, inhaling the wonderfully fragrant aroma of pine trees. She didn't think she'd ever get tired of that smell.

"So how much farther do we have to go?" she asked after a while.

"We should be able to get to a cabin I know of early tomorrow afternoon," he replied casually.

"A cabin?" She perked up a little. "Is it on Hank's land?"

He shook his head. It was on his land, but he couldn't tell her that. "It belongs to the neighboring ranch. It has a radio, if it still works."

"A radio? As in a listen-to-music radio, or a transmitting radio?"

"The transmitting kind."

"Oh." She swallowed uncomfortably. He didn't have to explain it any more. When they got to the cabin, all they'd have to do was transmit to Hank's ranch or the neighbor's ranch, and someone would come for them. The end of their time together was clearly in sight. In twenty-four hours, she would very likely be fast asleep in one of Hank's beds, and her time with Brock would be nothing more than a memory. Fast asleep? No, on second thought she'd probably be wide awake thinking about the man now sitting next to her. She felt like crying.

She glanced at Brock and found him studying her with a look that carried several emotions, the most obvious one being—she was sure—regret. Had the days they'd spent together come to mean something to him as well? Was he as reluctant as she was to return to reality?

"Oh, Brock," she said laying her head on his shoulder. His arm went around her, and she snuggled close to him. "I don't think I'll be able to take it when we get to the ranch and you hate me again."

Who'll be hating whom? he wondered with a trace of remorse. In all probability, this would be the one chance he would have to discover the marvels of being intimate with her. Once they were at Hank's, she'd either never forgive him or she'd tire of country life and go home. The thought that she'd last on the ranch seemed an unlikely scenario. If he was a believer in fate, then he was left with no choice.

He put all his doubts, his worries and his uncertainties out of his mind. Tonight, they would have no yesterdays, no tomorrows. There was only now, only her, and the stirring feelings he had that he was unable to name. Passion, too long denied and too consuming to ignore, would guide them through this night. The morning would bring its own set of problems, but morning was a lifetime away.

He tipped Jami's head back and claimed her mouth in a possessive kiss. "Then let me love you tonight."

She pressed her lips against the side of his neck. She couldn't have said no even if she wanted to. She knew it was now or never, and she couldn't face the prospect of it being never. A wave of tiny tremors swam through her.

"Yes," she whispered. "Yes."

Brock peeled off his jacket, then hers, and dropped them. Then he laid Jami on the fabric. He stretched out beside her and trailed his hand slowly down from her ear to her thigh. He felt her tremble in response, and his hand became unsteady from the depth of his desire. Then he brought his hand up to toy with a strand of her silky hair, spellbound by its softness. The scent of her floral soap filled the air around her.

"You smell like lilacs," he told her huskily.

She giggled. "So do you."

He let that remark slide. "I wonder just how good a job you did with that soap." He lifted the shirt she was wearing to reveal her stomach. "For instance, would I still smell those lilacs if I kissed you right here?" His mouth dropped to nibble her bare skin, and he was instantly rewarded by the contraction of her stomach muscles from the light contact. "Mmm, yes, there's lilacs here, too."

Her hands gripped his shoulders before drifting to massage the steely chords of his neck. "I'll bet you can find those lilacs a few other places, too."

"That's a bet I'm willing to take you up on, princess." He pulled her shirt off, and his lips followed the trail of lace that surrounded her breasts.

"Why do you keep calling me that?" she asked suddenly.

"Princess?" He raised his head to study her face thoughtfully. "I don't know. It just seems to fit you."

"But most of the time when you say it, it doesn't sound very complimentary."

"Well," he said, considering her words, "sometimes being a princess isn't a very good thing. Other times, it's great. Like now."

Her fingers reached up to skim the chiseled surface of his cheek. "And right now you're my prince."

"No. I'm never a prince. Right now I'm just a sneaking rogue who stole into the palace to ravage the king's daughter." His hand covered one of her breasts, and he kneaded the tiny tip until it became as hard as a pebble.

She arched against him and half laughed, half moaned. "You're right. You are more of a rogue than a prince. But you're still my hero."

"I like that," he decided. "Even though I don't deserve it." His mouth dipped to conquer her lips again, effectively cutting off conversation.

Her fingertips were itching to explore his bare skin, and she jerked his shirt free from the waistband of his jeans. Both hands roamed beneath the thin cotton, grazing the contours of his brawny pectorals, which she'd only been able to caress with her eyes earlier that day. Brock groaned and in one swift motion removed his shirt. Her bra was quick to follow, and as lace floated down to cover cotton, Brock lowered his naked chest to scorchingly meld with hers.

"You are exquisite," he murmured into her ear. "Simply exquisite."

She sighed blissfully. Never in her most fanciful imagination could she have dreamed he'd feel so wonderful. "You're not so bad yourself."

He rolled over suddenly, carrying her with him so that she ended up on top of him. One booted heel rubbed slowly up and down the back of her leg, alternating tempo with the gentle thrust of his hips.

"Jami?"

"Hmm?"

"Our jeans have got to go."

"I couldn't agree more."

They helped each other free from the final barriers that had prevented total contact of fevered flesh to fevered flesh.

Rock-hard planes molded with soft curves as pulses raced and desires raged. The sounds of chirping crickets and screeching owls permeated the clear night air.

Brock's hands stroked every inch of her, teasing here, seeking there, while his mouth covered first one taut breast and then the other, his tongue swirling around the rosy tips. Hunger gnawed in his loins, sharper and more ravishing than any he'd ever experienced. When his fingers finally moved to explore the sensitized recesses of her womanhood, her hands gripped his shoulders, and she immediately trembled and moved urgently against him.

She was on fire. Every nerve ending in her body tingled, every pore ached for his touch. Need overpowered reason, spiraled tighter and demanded release. She thought she would die if he didn't stop soon; she thought she would die if he ever stopped at all.

He wanted to make it last for her so that as long as she lived, she would never forget this night. But the last shreds of his control were almost shattered; so with his knees he edged her legs apart and joined with her in one blazing plunge. She matched his rhythm with equal strength and ardor as the intensity built higher, then higher still, until they were both thrown over the edge in uncontrollable rapture. They clung to each other for a long time, until their shaking bodies and wild heartbeats calmed.

At last Brock shifted and tucked her snugly against him. She kissed his sweat-glistened chest. "I never knew," she said simply.

"Knew what?"

"That making love could be so...." Her voice trailed off as she searched for a word to describe it. "So complete." Suddenly embarrassed, she glanced at him. Maybe she was being foolish. Maybe he hadn't been as overwhelmed as she was. One look at his face convinced her otherwise.

"Yeah, it was pretty great, wasn't it?" His voice was casual, but his eyes told her he meant that and more. "And you know what they say," he prompted with a grin.

"What?"

"It's even better the second time."

"Really?" She didn't see how it could be, but she played along anyway. "How about the third time?"

"Better yet."

Her smile faded slightly. "We only have tonight, you know."

"I know, but the night is still young."

"That's true. And I've heard the nights are pretty long out here."

"That's a fact. Maybe we can even sleep late tomorrow morning. That is," he said as his hand started roaming over her, "if we get to sleep at all."

Goose bumps rose on her skin as her fingers traced patterns in the thick black hair on his chest. "Who needs sleep, anyway?"

Proving that neither of them did, they made love again before dozing off, only to wake and discover passion flaring once more. It was near dawn before their bodies were satisfied and spent enough to allow them to sleep for a few hours.

"There it is," Brock said, pointing.

Jami's gaze followed his outstretched arm until she found the outline of a small cabin set amid tall, straight trees in the side of the mountain. It was still at least a mile away, but she already felt choked by its presence. "I see it," she said, her voice irritatingly unsteady.

Brock squeezed her hand reassuringly. "Everything will work out."

She could only nod. They both knew that wasn't true, but neither was willing to admit it.

Their relationship had been different as soon as they'd gotten up. Jami couldn't keep her eyes off Brock, and every time she looked at him, she saw he was watching her, too. When they'd eaten a leisurely breakfast, they couldn't sit close enough together. They rarely laughed all morning, seldom even smiled at each other. Rather, they kissed often, touched more. Everything they did had an air of desperation about it, as if every second together would be their last. They'd traveled slowly all day, stopping often to rest and simply hold each other.

Now, staring at the cabin, Jami felt frozen to the spot. Last night had been so perfect, and it was hard to accept that what she'd shared with Brock would never happen again. Even if it did, it wouldn't be the same.

"Come on," Brock urged quietly, pulling her along.

She followed, holding his hand for all she was worth, and tried not to cry. It took them an hour to cross a distance that should've only taken them twenty minutes.

Jami stood in front of the cabin while Brock located the key in a knothole in one of the logs of the wall. He opened the door, and they stepped inside.

"It's nice," she said, her eyes taking in the clean interior of the cabin. It was small and cozy, tastefully decorated with simple furniture. "Who did you say owned it?"

Brock cleared his throat. "It's owned by the Jacoby ranch." Without another word, he walked to the radio that was sitting on a wooden stand in the kitchen. After only a moment of adjusting the various dials, the radio crackled to life.

Jami sank on a sofa that was surprisingly soft and listened to Brock transmit a message over and over into the handset. In about ten minutes, an excited voice invaded their privacy through the radio. Brock told the man where they were, said they were both fine and asked the man to send a truck for them right away. When he was through, he came and sat next to Jami on the sofa.

"How long will it take?" she asked finally.

"About an hour, I imagine." He put his arm around her shoulders and kissed her forehead. "That awful bruise is almost gone."

"Thank goodness. I was having a hard time trying to keep it covered up."

"You didn't have to bother. Every inch of you is beautiful, bruises or no bruises."

As she rested her head against his chest, her eyes drifted through the one interior door in the cabin. From her position on the sofa, she had a perfect view of the bed that loomed so large in the other room. Her stomach tightened at the symbol of reality staring her in the face. If circumstances were different, she and Brock might be in that bed right now. As it was, the bed served as a nagging reminder of how things had already changed between them. She closed her eyes, blocking out the sight, but she could not as easily block out the memories.

Brock felt the tension in her, and though he guessed the cause, he didn't know what to do about it. He entwined his fingers with hers and brought her hand to his lips. There was so much he wanted to say to her, so much he should say.

It was only at this minute that he was fully realizing what an idiot he'd been not to have told Jami long ago who he really was. How could he have made such a gross error in judgment? At first, it had been like a game to him, letting her think what she wanted to. He had thought she would not be able to handle looking like a fool when they returned to the ranch and she found out how wrong she'd been about him. He'd thought maybe that would help get rid of her. He still didn't want her to have Hank's ranch, that hadn't changed a bit. But his opinion of her had. She was stubborn and strong enough to stick around just to spite him. A couple days ago, that would have merely annoyed him. But today, it was tearing him apart.

She'd hate him for not telling her the truth. She'd stay to take over Hank's ranch, and she wouldn't have anything to do with him. At this point, he couldn't decide which part of that bothered him the most. The fact that he couldn't acknowledge his feelings only strengthened his belief that he'd gotten far too involved with Jami for his own good. He hadn't wanted to. Hell, he didn't even know how it happened.

But it had. And it was too late to do anything about it. Just like it was too late to tell her the truth. He wished he could, he really did. He knew it would be better for her to hear it now, not later. But he was a damn coward, because all the words died in his throat every time he tried to get them out.

So they simply sat together in silence. When they heard the faint sound of an engine approaching, Brock stood and pulled Jami up in front of him. After crushing her in a fierce embrace, he loosened his hold enough to kiss her with soft tenderness. She hung onto him until the truck's engine grew so loud they knew the truck was right outside. They broke away from each other then, picked up their meager belongings and went out to meet their rescuer.

"Brock!" A man several years younger than Jami yelled a greeting as soon as they came out the door. "God, man, it's great to see you! We were all so worried. But you don't look any worse for the wear. And you must be Jamaica McKenzie. You look good, too."

"Please call me Jami," she said, blushing slightly as the man appraised her while he pumped her hand in a strong handshake.

"Jami, why don't you hop in the truck?" Brock suggested curtly. "Sam, come on over here and help me lock up the cabin."

Jami winced at Brock's tone of voice. It had been a long time since she'd heard him talk that way. They weren't even at the ranch, and already she felt that the man she was in love with was a stranger. In love? No, she couldn't be. She couldn't have let herself go that far, could she? Maybe she was just a little confused right now. She'd get over these silly emotions as soon as she got to Hank's. *Sure she would.* Jami sighed heavily. It was futile to deny it. She had it bad.

She stepped into the truck, and was followed a minute later by the two men. Brock climbed in through the driver's side and scooted over to sit next to her while Sam got behind the wheel. They bumped halfway down the mountain making their own road as they went until they finally reached a gravel path. Jami dozed off then, suddenly very weary, her head dropping to Brock's shoulder.

In what seemed like no time at all, Brock was shaking her awake. She opened her eyes to discover they were in front of her grandfather's ranch house. It hadn't changed at all in fifteen years, which was somehow comforting. Its white exterior was accented by black shutters, with a porch that ran along the whole length of the house. Even the old porch swing was still in the same place, in the western corner where a person could watch the sunset. Green shrubs dotted the front lawn, but they were much bigger than she remembered.

Several men approached the truck before she got up the nerve to get out. Then the front door of the house swung open, and there stood her grandfather.

From that distance, the only difference she could see in him was that he was thinner. Her limbs finally sprang into action, and she jumped out of the truck and ran to him. He opened his arms to her, and she hugged him tightly.

Hank pushed her away after a moment, and sharp eyes studied her. "You look good, girl. A little skinny, maybe, but all right."

"I could say the same about you." She took a closer look at him, and was dismayed to notice the hollows in his once robust cheeks, the sunken eyes, the slight stoop. He looked older than his years, and very tired. "I'm sorry if you were worried about me," she told him, wishing she could attribute his appearance to a few days of anguish over her. But she knew that wasn't it. If he hadn't been in poor health, he never would have sent for her.

"Worry?" he scoffed. "Why should I worry? You were with Brock, weren't you?" But the slight moistness in his eyes gave him away. His gaze left his granddaughter to look at the truck. "Come up here, Brock. I want to thank you for looking after Jami."

Jami glanced at Brock, who was making his way rather reluctantly to them. His gaze was unwaveringly on her. An inexplicable twinge of uneasiness went through her.

"I don't know how to thank you," Hank was saying as he shook Brock's hand. "And you don't know how glad I am to see you safe, too. I don't know what I would've done if I'd lost two of the most important people in my life in one swipe."

Jami smiled fondly at her grandfather, touched by his words. He'd never been one to show much affection or sentiment. She was a bit surprised to have him include Brock in that rare bit of emotion. Why would one of his cowhands be so important to him?

"Your granddaughter is one tough lady, Hank," Brock said. "You should be proud of her."

"I am," Hank replied. "Well, Brock, I won't keep you any longer. I'm sure you want to get home. Why don't you come for supper tomorrow night? If you're up to it, that is. Helena can fix you up your favorite meal as another way of showing my appreciation."

"Sure, Hank." He started to walk down the porch steps. "That sounds great. You know I can't pass up Helena's cooking. See you tomorrow night." The last sentence he tossed at Jami with a tiny smile.

"Wait a minute!" Brock stopped, and Jami looked from him to Hank and back to Brock again. "Will someone please tell me what's going on here?"

"What do you mean?" Hank asked in obvious confusion.

"Doesn't Brock live on the ranch?"

"Of course not, Jami." Hank gave his granddaughter a look that clearly stated he thought she must be a little distraught from her ordeal and not thinking normally. "Brock Jacoby doesn't live on my ranch."

"Jacoby?" she repeated with a frown. She'd heard that name before. But where?

"Yes, Jacoby. Brock owns the ranch that adjoins this one. In fact, it's even bigger than mine."

"You mean he doesn't work for you?" she said, her emerald eyes piercing into Brock's steady gaze.

"Good heaven's no, girl," Hank chortled. "He's one of the richest ranchers in the state."

Jami could only stare in disbelief at Brock. She couldn't think of a thing to say.

Brock decided then and there to get out while the getting was good. "See you both tomorrow night," he called despite the severe tightening in his chest.

Jami watched him jump into the truck. In seconds he had disappeared in a cloud of dust.

Seven

—

Jami felt like she'd been slapped in the face. Or punched in the stomach. Or worse.

How could he have done this to her?

Hank cleared his throat uncomfortably. "Jami, come on," he urged gruffly. "Lets go inside."

She turned in a daze and followed her grandfather into his surprisingly modern home. He must have remodeled since she'd been here. The living room was still decorated in pleasant earth tones, but the sofa and chairs were of over-stuffed, contemporary design. Several large plants brightened the room, adding a homey touch that she didn't remember being there before. Even the scuffed hardwood floors had been covered with thick, multicolored carpet.

"This room is beautiful," she said with a smile that was only partially forced. Maybe if she tried hard enough, she could keep her mind on the changes around her instead of on the way Brock had lied to her. "When did you redo it?"

"Last year. Helena helped me pick everything out. She
said it was high time the place looked livable again, that it
needed a woman's touch."

As if on cue, Jami heard footsteps approaching from the
kitchen. Her gaze rested on the heavy woman rushing toward her. At least she hadn't changed, Jami thought with
relief. Her kind eyes still twinkled merrily, her hair was still
the same shade of ash blond, and she still wore housedresses with matching slippers. The next thing she knew,
Jami was wrapped in Helena's burly arms.

"Jami, thank God! We were all so worried about you."
The older woman released Jami to carefully scrutinize her,
as if assuring herself Jami was all right. "When the search
plane Hank sent out couldn't find a trace of you, we didn't
know what to think."

"Search plane?" She and Brock had never noticed a
plane. "When did you send out a search plane?"

"The day after you didn't show up," Hank said. "I had
a man looking for you all afternoon."

"It rained that day. I guess we couldn't hear or see a plane
in the storm."

"I figured as much, but I still had to have someone look.
I could only get the pilot for that one day. I'd arranged for
another search plane today, but it didn't turn out to be necessary."

"If you'd been with anyone else besides Brock," Helena
put in, "I'm sure we all would've given up on you having
any chance of being alive."

Jami's smile turned into a bitter smirk. It seemed everyone had a bad case of hero worship for Brock. If she
wouldn't come across looking like such a fool, she would tell
them all what a rat he really was. "Yes," she replied in a
deceivingly sweet voice, "he was most helpful in the wilderness. He took very good care of me."

"Come on, dear," Helena said as she put her arm around
Jami's slender shoulders. "I'll show you to your room.
You'd probably like to wash up and change before you come
down to the kitchen for a nice hot meal."

Jami let Helena usher her up the stairs and into the bedroom she'd occupied as a child. This room, like the living room, had been completely redone.

"Oh, Helena," she breathed in awe, "this is lovely." Her eyes eagerly took in the large room, which was decorated in shades of gold and pale orange. There was a lacy, flowered comforter on the queen-size bed, with matching frilly curtains on the three windows. The immense oak dressers appeared to be brand new, and the oak-spindled rocking chair near one of the windows looked very inviting. An even plusher carpet than the one in the living room warmed the floor beneath her feet. A huge bouquet of fresh flowers adorned the nightstand by the bed.

"I'm glad you like it," Helena said, obviously pleased with Jami's reaction.

"But why did Hank do all this?" Jami asked in bewilderment. Her grandfather had always poured his money into his barns and the grounds, and he'd never cared about the way the house looked. He used to say the only time he was inside was when he ate or slept, so there was no need to keep everything fancy when it was used so little.

The older woman shrugged. "It's no secret that he wants you to take over the ranch. I told him you'd never want to live in this house the way it was. It took me a few months of preaching, but I finally got through to him."

Jami was stunned. "You mean he did all this for me? He remodeled his whole house just on the chance that I would agree to run the ranch?"

"Well, let's just say he hoped, it would help influence your decision," Helena admitted. "I'll leave you alone now, dear. Come down to the kitchen whenever you're ready."

Jami stood in the doorway for a long time after Helena left. After days of staring at trees, dirt, weeds and rocks, to be in such a sunny, feminine room felt heavenly. At last she kicked off her shoes and padded over to the bed. What she wouldn't give to lie down on its softness for even a little while, but she was too dirty, and she didn't want to soil the

spread. She crossed the room and entered the adjoining
bathroom.

She turned on the shower until hot steam filled the room,
then eagerly pulled off her clothes and stepped into the tub.
She closed her eyes in ecstasy as the hot water washed over
her tired, aching body. Hot water. It was a wonderful convenience that she would appreciate from now on.

Memories of her last bathing drifted into her mind. She
had to admit, washing in the river had been an experience,
one that she had enjoyed. She couldn't help remembering
how stunning Brock had looked after his turn in the river,
and traitorous goose bumps rose on her skin as she thought
about it.

"Damn him!" she cursed. But she refused to think about
him more. She wouldn't let thoughts of him spoil her
shower. She grabbed the bar of soap from the built-in shelf,
and had to also use it to wash her hair since there was no
shampoo.

She lathered and rinsed herself quickly, for despite her
resolve, memories of the last time she had been naked under
Brock's hard body had ruined what should've been a luxu-
rious shower. The only way she could get the haunting
thoughts out of her mind was to get some clothes on. Fast.

She jumped out of the tub and stood dripping on the bath
mat while she opened several cabinet doors searching for
towels. Finally she found them, and she wrapped one
around her hair and one around her body. A sinking suspicion was starting to grow in her mind as she quickly pulled
open one drawer after another in the vanity. All were empty.

Jami leaned against the bathroom door and felt like
laughing hysterically at the irony of it all. Naturally, her
grandfather had expected her to bring all her own toiletries
and hadn't stocked any for her. Only now did it occur to her
that her overnight case had been forgotten in the back of
Brock's truck. She had nothing, not even clothes, except for
those she'd been wearing. Here she was, in the civilized
world, and she had fewer personal belongings than she'd
had out in the wild.

As she emerged from the bathroom, still dressed in the towels, there was a knock at her door. She called for whoever it was to come in and was shocked when Helena entered the bedroom carrying her overnight case.

"Where—where did you get that?"

"Brock dropped it off a few minutes ago," a beaming Helena announced. "He said he was halfway to his ranch before he realized you'd left it behind. He thought you might need it, so he came back with it. Such a thoughtful man, that Brock. And a handsome devil, too, don't you think?"

Jami took the case from Helena, ignoring the compliments to the man she had more descriptive words for than thoughtful and handsome. Devil was a little closer to the mark. "Thank you, Helena. I do need this desperately, but I need clean clothes even more. I don't suppose there are any women's clothes around here, are there?"

"I keep a couple extra housedresses in the spare room, but since I don't sleep here, I'm afraid I don't have much. Of course, you're welcome to one of them, if you can stand wearing it."

"Anything would be better than putting on dirty clothes," Jami assured her.

"If you want to give me your things, I'll get them in the washer right away," Helena offered.

"I can do it myself later, if you'll show me how." She figured it was high time she started taking care of herself.

"I can show you another day if you want, after you rest up a bit. For now, just let me do it for you."

"Okay, that would be great." Jami dumped her sodden clothes from the overnight case and retrieved the ones she'd been wearing from the bathroom. She handed the bundle to Helena.

"I'll be right back with that dress. In a couple of hours, you'll be in your own clothes."

Ten minutes later, clad in one of Helena's tents, Jami was seated at the vanity in her bathroom, carefully sorting out her cosmetics and toiletries. She couldn't help but wonder what Brock's real motivation was in bringing her overnight case. Was he being considerate, knowing how much these few things meant to her? She doubted it. Rather, she thought it was his mocking way of showing her how materialistic she was. He thought she was still shallow and vain.

Jami frowned at her reflection. Brock was wrong if he thought she hadn't changed during their time together. She even looked different. Older, somehow, and a little more real. And something else, something she couldn't quite yet put her finger on. Was there a cynical gleam to her eyes now? Or was it determination?

Just then her stomach growled loudly, putting an end to her self-examination. She was ravenously hungry, and the thought of real food waiting downstairs drove her to her feet. Barefoot, wearing Helena's baggy dress with absolutely nothing under it, she headed to the kitchen.

The housekeeper took one look at Jami and burst out laughing. "That dress doesn't do a whole lot for you, does it? No matter, it's clean. Have a seat, dear, and I'll fix you something."

Jami dropped into one of the wooden chairs by the round table in the corner. "Looks to me like this room has been a bit modernized, too," she observed. "I'm sure the microwave is new, and Hank didn't have an electric stove before, did he? Or a dishwasher."

Helena sighed. "No, you're right. It's all new. And it's taken me a good while to get the hang of using the oven. The microwave still scares me, so I don't use that, and I'll never be convinced a dishwasher gets dishes cleaner than I do."

"Then why did you let Hank get all these things?"

"It's like I told you earlier. They're all for you. Hank figured you couldn't cook in a kitchen with antique appliances, so he replaced everything."

"Well, the joke's on him, then. I can't cook, period. New appliances or not."

"You mean you don't know how to run a microwave?" Helena asked, crestfallen.

Jami shook her head. "Sorry. That's what my parents had a cook for."

"Oh, my."

"But I'd like to learn," Jami assured the older woman quickly. "I guess a twenty-seven-year-old woman should be able to cook herself something simple in a microwave in this day and age, don't you think?"

"I surely do. We can learn to use that foolish thing together. Now, what would you like to eat?"

"Anything. No, make that everything. Really, whatever's handy will be fine."

While Helena was busy taking things out of the refrigerator, Hank walked into the kitchen. His eyes rested briefly on his granddaughter, then he sat beside her.

"You look very refreshed," he said. "How are you feeling?"

"A little tired," she admitted. "And very hungry. But otherwise I'm fine."

"Are you sure?"

"Of course," Jami answered cautiously. Her grandfather's intense scrutiny was making her a little nervous. He was looking at her like her father had when—her father! She'd forgotten all about her parents. "Have you called my mother and father yet and told them I was all right? I should have thought of that right away." She was glancing around the kitchen for a phone when Hank noisily cleared his throat.

"I never told your parents that you didn't arrive on schedule," Hank said quietly.

"What?" Jami stared at him in disbelief. "You lied to them? But why?"

Hank looked away from Jami's demanding gaze. "I knew, being with Brock, that you had to be all right. You just had to be. But your father never would've understood that."

"My father is also your son," she reminded him harshly. "I know you two haven't spoken in years, and I think it's about time you tell me why."

Hank shook his head. ''I don't want to get into all of that with you tonight. You've been through a great deal, and you need time to rest. I don't want to burden you with too many things before you're ready.''

''I'm ready now!''

''Hank, maybe you should tell her tonight,'' Helena intervened. ''She does have a right to know. And now that you opened up the can of worms, she's going to die of curiosity all night if you don't tell her.''

''That's right, I will,'' Jami added.

Hank sighed and nodded. ''Very well. I'll tell you everything.''

More than an hour had passed since Jami had returned to her room. She was exhausted and numb, yet her eyes would not remain closed. Too much had happened in the past twenty-four hours for her to unwind. Irritated with herself, she got out of bed and sat in the rocker. Tucking one bare foot underneath her, she propped her other foot against the windowsill and used it to set the rocker into a gentle, soothing motion.

The discussion she'd had with Hank had certainly explained a great deal, but it had also given her a lot to think about. Finally hearing the reason her father and Hank hadn't spoken for so long had left her uneasy, to say the least. She still thought there must be more to the story that Hank was leaving out, but she supposed he'd told her the biggest part.

Hank's land contained one of the biggest oilfields in the state of Montana, or so he said he'd been told. And her father wanted the land so he could drill for oil. It was as simple as that. Or was it? She'd gotten the feeling something else was involved, and someday she would get Hank to tell her the rest. For now, she knew what most of the big dissension was between the two men. Hank had always made his money in livestock and wanted more than anything to preserve the natural beauty of his land. The odd thing about it all was, she understood his position. And agreed with him.

Of course, the real blow had been hearing Hank's plans for his ranch if she didn't want it or couldn't make a go of it. The ranch would go to Brock. Hank's will made it official, and if she decided to bow out before her grandfather died, he said he would sell it outright to Brock.

If that hadn't been a bitter pill to swallow! Gradually, everything had become clear to her. Brock wanted Hank's ranch, and for him to get it, she had to be out of the picture. By showing her the harshness of the Montana countryside, and by pointing out how she didn't belong here, he'd been trying to get her to go back home.

But Brock didn't care about the oil, Hank had told her. She'd asked him point-blank why he didn't think Brock would drill on his property. After all, she reasoned, even if he did own Hank's ranch, he would most likely still live on his own. He'd never have to look at the oil rigs if he didn't want to. All he would have to do was sit back and let the money pour in. She'd mentioned as much to Hank.

Her grandfather's answer had been quick and harsh. "Now, you listen to me, girl," he'd said, his voice barely under control. "You haven't been around this place in— how many years? Ten? Fifteen? You don't know anything about what goes on around here. And you obviously didn't learn much about Brock while you were stranded with him, or you would never think to ask such a question."

She'd tried to protest, but Hank had risen awkwardly and walked stiffly to the kitchen door. At the last minute, he'd turned back.

"I'm glad you're here and I'm glad you're safe," he told her gruffly. "Your future is in your hands. I've laid my cards on the table. But don't ever question my judgment of the men around here. I didn't get where I am today by not knowing people. Your decision to take over the ranch or not has nothing to do with Brock or what you might think he's going to do with my land. That decision is mine, and I've made it. Good night."

Your decision to take over the ranch or not has nothing to do with Brock. Hank's words echoed in her head. How wrong he was! If she went back to New York, the ranch would become Brock's. After the way he'd deceived her, he didn't deserve it. Even if he wouldn't spoil the land by drilling for oil, he still didn't deserve it.

Suddenly restless, she got up and walked into the bathroom. She gazed at her troubled reflection in the mirror and groaned softly. Brock knew her well, she had to admit to herself. He'd known just how to get to her. He'd left her confused, full of doubts and resentful.

And still she loved him. Still she wanted him.

She longed to shake the feelings of desire completely from her body, but even now as the vivid memories of their special night together were relived in her mind, she couldn't keep a severe ache from forming deep inside her. The thought that she would never again experience that harmony of two bodies perfectly suited to one another was so distressing she didn't dare dwell on it.

Jami wandered into the bedroom and pulled out the covers on the bed again. She slipped between the sheets and drew the comforter up to her chin. The bed felt wonderful, and she was dead tired. So why wouldn't her body give in and go to sleep?

She'd predicted this last night, she realized crossly. She knew once she got to the ranch, she'd be laying awake, thinking of Brock. Wishing he was there with her. *So she could give him a piece of her mind!* She sighed. *And then she would give him her body.*

She was surprised at herself for feeling this way, she really was. When Jonathon had betrayed her, she'd never wanted to see him again. So why did she still yearn for Brock? Why hadn't she learned her lesson three years ago? Would she ever learn?

Oh, she would learn, all right, she told herself with firm resolution. She would learn about running this ranch. She had nothing better to do with her life anyway, so why not live here? She could run a cattle and horse ranch if she put her mind to it. Couldn't she?

Actually, she had no idea if she could, because she'd never set her mind to anything in her life, at least not to anything of any importance. But she had Hank's blood in her, as well as her father's, so there had to be some successful genes in her somewhere. All she had to do was find them.

But first, she had to get some sleep. She wasn't very successful in that endeavor. It was several hours before her whirling mind and restless body eased enough for her to relax. When sleep did claim her at last, it was fitfully interrupted with all too pleasant dreams of a certain rugged cowboy with a silver tongue and gentle hands.

Early the next morning, Jami found Hank and Helena in the kitchen drinking coffee together. Dressed in her jeans and shirt, she felt more like herself, despite the lack of a good night's rest. Helena jumped up as she joined them at the table.

"Good morning!" the housekeeper greeted her cheerily. "Would you like some coffee?"

"Yes, thank you," Jami answered, eyeing her grandfather cautiously. She wondered if he was still upset over her question about Brock the night before.

Finally Hank met her gaze and merely nodded his acknowledgment of her presence. "You look tired," he observed after a few minutes. "Didn't you sleep well?"

Jami looked away quickly, afraid he would see right into her mind and view the sensual dreams she'd had about Brock. "I slept fine," she lied. She picked up the cup of coffee Helena had set down and took a sip. It tasted more like water than coffee. Of course, considering the strong, thick brew she'd been drinking for the past few days, that was no wonder.

"What would you like for breakfast, dear?"

"Whatever's easiest, Helena," Jami told her. While the housekeeper was bustling around the kitchen, her grandfather remained silent. Finally unable to bear the tension between them any longer, she decided she should apologize. "I'm sorry about last night," she began quietly.

Hank's sharp eyes looked into hers for a long moment, then softened. "That's okay. Maybe I overreacted a little. But if you're going to learn how to run this place properly, you can't be challenging my decisions."

"I wasn't really challenging you. I was just asking a question that I needed to know the answer to." She favored the old man with an easy grin. "How can I learn everything without asking questions?"

Hank grunted. "Some questions are good to ask. Some aren't."

"Well, I'll just have to learn that distinction, too, won't I?"

"It sounds like maybe you've made up your mind."

"I think I have." She took a deep breath. "I've decided to stay and take you up on your generous offer."

"I'm so glad, Jami. You're the only McKenzie who could come close to feeling what I do for this ranch. I found that out when you were here just that one summer. For some fool reason, it's always been my wish to leave the ranch to someone in my family, someone who can carry on the heritage. I only hope I didn't wait too long to send for you, that I have enough time left to teach you everything you need to know."

"Actually, I think your timing in asking me out here was just about perfect," Jami commented dryly, and she knew that was the truth. Six months or a year ago, she never would have considered the idea.

"Well, so be it," Hank said, firmly putting his coffee cup down. "I'll go call Griffin up here, and you can get started right away."

"You'll do no such thing, Hank McKenzie!" Helena protested immediately. "You let the girl have one day to settle in. Besides, we've got to go to town today and get her the things she had to leave on your plane."

Hank tipped his head thoughtfully, smiling affectionately at Helena. "Let this be your first lesson, Jami," he said with mock brusqueness. "If you don't put this old bat in her place once in a while, she'll think she runs you, and the next thing you know, she'll have taken over."

"Old bat!" Helena screeched, cuffing Hank on the shoulder. "Why, you old coot, who're you calling an old bat?"

"All right, all right, you win this time," Hank conceded with a chuckle. "Jami can have the day off today. But don't be too long in town. You know Brock's coming for supper, and he's expecting his favorite meal. And don't burn it this time!"

"Burn it!" Helena exploded in outrage. "Jami, don't you listen to a word this old codger says. I've never burned a meal in my life!"

Jami was glad neither one of them was waiting for her comment, because her heart was suddenly pounding too loudly for her to manage any response. She'd forgotten Brock was going to be there for supper. She passed off the thrill that gave her as anxiousness to tell him just what she thought of him. Not to mention the pleasure she would get informing him that she was taking over the ranch and he'd never get it.

She supposed they would expect her to be civil to Brock all through dinner, too. "Ha!" she exclaimed, unaware she'd spoken out loud until both Hank and Helena turned toward her. Hank's expression was puzzled, while Helena's was downright hurt.

"You don't believe me?" Helena said, a bit perturbed. "Honestly, I've never burned anything in my life."

"Oh, no!" Jami said quickly, blushing at Helena's misinterpretation. "I didn't mean that at all. I know you're a wonderful cook. My mind was on something else altogether. Really, it had nothing to do with what you said."

Helena frowned, obviously unconvinced. Hank, however, seemed amused by the whole thing. "As soon as you're done eating, why don't you walk down to the barns while Helena gets ready to take you to town?" he suggested. "Look up Griffin, and—"

"Griffin!" Jami interrupted in surprise. The name had slipped by her moments before. "Griffin still works for you?" She remembered the crusty old foreman from when she'd visited the ranch as a child. The man had the patience of a saint with animals, but not with horse-crazy girls. Still, she knew she'd gotten under his skin by the end of her summer there. The day she'd ridden Hank's best stallion as well as any of his cowhands, Griffin had given her an uncharacteristic bear hug and told her how proud he was of her. Hearing he was still around brought on a welcome surge of hopefulness.

"Yeah, he's still here. The old fool will be here until he dies, just like me. Anyway, as I was saying, go find him, and there's another old friend of yours down there, too."

"Another old friend?" Jami repeated. "Who?"

But Hank only winked and patted her hand. "You'll see. Just ask Griffin. He'll show you."

Fifteen minutes later, Jami was strolling slowly through the biggest of Hank's barns. She'd forgotten what a pleasant smell a clean barn had; the mixture of sweet hay and the unique smell of horses combined to form one of the best natural odors in the world. She patted each and every nose that pushed out over the stall doors to greet her. When she was almost to the end of the first row, she stopped dead in front of one of the stalls.

"No, it couldn't be," she whispered reverently. Goose bumps rose on her flesh, and she felt as if she was stepping back in time to her childhood. She stared in disbelief at the lovely white Arabian mare inside the stall. "Moondust? Is it really you?" she asked the horse. The mare nickered an answer, coming up to her at once and thrusting her velvety nose into Jami's chest.

"It is you!" Jami said, laughing and crying all at once. She opened the stall door and slipped inside. She put her arms around the horse's neck and hugged her tightly. As she did, Moondust rubbed her chin across Jami's back.

"I just can't believe it," she told the mare. "Let me look at you." She moved back and studied the horse and was delighted to see she was in such good health. She stepped forward again and ran her hands lovingly over the mare's neck, back and sides.

"Still looks the same, don't she? You sure have changed, though."

Jami jumped at the sound of a man's voice from outside the stall. She didn't have to look at the speaker to identify him. "Griffin!" She turned and grinned at him. "It's so good to see you, too. You look great."

Griffin whistled. "I might say the same about you. What happened to my favorite little girl in pigtails?"

"She grew up. Although, looking at you and this lady, I feel like I'm a kid again." She gazed at Moondust and softly scratched the horse's neck while a summer full of wonderful memories flew to her. She'd practically lived on this horse's back. The gentle mare had patiently put up with her clumsiness while she'd learned how to ride. Even though Hank and Griffin had insisted she ride every horse on the place to get the best experience each individual horse could teach her, none had found a place in her heart like Moondust.

"She remembers you," Griffin said, slightly in awe. "Sure as shoot, even though it's been years and years, she remembers you."

"She must be getting old by now," Jami said, secretly pleased at Griffin's words. "She's got to be in her twenties."

"Don't tell her that. She still thinks she's a young filly. Acts like one most of the time, too."

"I wish I had time to ride her right now," Jami said wistfully. "But I've got to go into town with Helena. Maybe I can take her out when we get back." She reluctantly left the stall and turned her attention to Griffin.

She was amazed that he had aged so well. His hair was still the same shade of light brown, still cut in an unfashionable crew cut. He was as thin as she remembered him, but she knew his muscles, although barely visible, were sinewy and strong. His face was a darker shade of brown than his hair, and deeply lined. Hazel eyes that could turn mischievous or harsh were twinkling at her.

"It's good to see you here, missy," Griffin told her earnestly. "Has Hank talked to you yet about, uh, things?"

"About taking over the ranch?" Jami said bluntly.

"Yeah."

She nodded. "And I'm going to give it a shot." Griffin remained silent, evidently waiting for her to say something more. Jami took a deep, steadying breath. She knew her next words would be very important to her success on the ranch and with the foreman. "I know that after my grandfather is gone, technically I'll be in charge. But I want you to know that I'll rely on you to advise me about everything. I don't know how valuable all the other men who work here are, but I do know that I'll never be able to do it without you staying on and remaining the indisputable boss."

She wasn't merely flattering him, she was speaking honestly. Griffin sensed that, and his face broke into a relieved smile. "No reason why a woman can't oversee a ranch. You'll learn quick enough how to do your part."

"Then you'll stay?"

"Of course. I've lived on this ranch so long it wouldn't feel like home anywhere else."

"Thanks, Griffin." Jami impulsively reached out and hugged him.

"Now, now, none of that, missy," he said, pushing her away after a moment. His eyes danced merrily. "We don't want any of the men to think we've got a thing going, you know."

Jami burst out laughing. "You're right," she agreed with mock seriousness. "I'll watch that from now on."

"Good." He laughed, too, and put his arm around her shoulder. "Come on, I'll show you the other horses."

The rest of the day passed quickly for Jami. Griffin ushered her around the barns for nearly an hour. Then she was whisked off in Helena's battered old car to go shopping. The trip to the nearest town took an hour and a half. Then they spent two hours visiting all the stores on Main Street. It wouldn't have taken them half as long if Helena hadn't stopped to talk to everyone they saw and introduced Jami.

They got home around three o'clock. While Helena started supper, Jami escaped to her room with her new purchases. She pondered about how much makeup to wear for Brock, then defiantly decided to do her face up like she was going to a fancy party with the most elite society. Picking an outfit proved a little more difficult. Finally she chose a flouncy denim skirt that came midway down her calves, new cowboy boots, a red and blue checked blouse and a wide red belt. She pulled one side of her long hair away from her face with a blue comb and put on dangly silver earrings.

"Not bad," she said approvingly to her reflection in the full-length mirror. She spun in a circle, liking the way her skirt twirled and swished around her legs.

As she headed down the stairs, she heard Brock's deep, rich voice coming from the kitchen. Her throat suddenly went dry, and her hands started shaking. Damn it, she was supposed to be mad at him, not excited to see him! she chastised herself. She alternately curled her fingers into fists and relaxed them, willing them to become steady. She paused near the bottom of the stairs, momentarily considering running to her bedroom to hide for the night. It was too soon to face him, too soon to...

"I'll go call her."

Jami heard Brock say the words and was a second too late in letting their meaning sink in. She was still frozen on the stairs when he walked out of the kitchen. The smile that had been on his face faded into something else when he saw her a moment later.

"I guess I don't have to call you after all," he said distractedly, his eyes raking over her slowly and hungrily.

"Call me what?" she quipped, despite the lump that had formed in her throat.

"Princess," he replied huskily. "That's what you look like right now."

She bit her lip, steeling herself against the tide of desire that was rushing through her body at the sight of him. He

was wearing jeans that hugged his lean hips and long legs
and a gray short-sleeved shirt that emphasized his broad
chest and muscular forearms. The scent of him—soap and
something else that was uniquely male and distinctly
Brock—drifted up to her, making her even dizzier.

"Well, do you know what you look like?" she asked, her
voice surprisingly cool.

"What?"

"A first-class jerk."

Eight

Brock was stunned. "What did you call me?"

"You heard me," Jami replied with deceptive calm. She walked down the rest of the stairs and grabbed his arm. "You come in here with me. I want to talk to you right now."

"Helena has dinner ready," he protested lamely. He wasn't looking forward to this scene at all, but he knew he had it coming. In fact, he'd been able to think of little else in the past twenty-four hours. Once he'd contented himself with the fact that everything had apparently gone smoothly on his ranch while he'd been away, his concentration had centered on Jami and the way she must be feeling about him. And how he felt about her. But how did he feel? A whole night of pacing around his bedroom hadn't helped enlighten him.

"Helena can wait." When she was satisfied he was going to follow her, she dropped his arm. The electrifying effect of touching him didn't help her nerves, but it did help to increase her anger. The trouble was, she didn't know who she was madder at: him for betraying her or herself for letting him.

When she opened the door to Hank's den and switched on the light, she had to stop momentarily and look around her. Although every other room in the house had been remodeled, this room hadn't changed one iota since she'd been here as a child. It was a man's room, plain and simple, filled with big, bold furniture in dark mahogany. Papers and magazines were stacked neatly all over Hank's desk and end tables. Pictures of all of his beloved prize Arabians adorned the paneled walls, while the hardwood floor was dark and shiny from a recent coating of wax. The ceiling-high bookcases that covered one wall were filled to capacity.

Brock sat on the leather couch near a large brick fireplace. "So what do you want to talk about?"

She dropped into an easy chair that faced the couch and crossed her legs. Her upraised foot tapped agitatedly in the air. "I think you owe me an explanation. And an apology."

"I haven't done one thing to you that I'm sorry for."

"Oh, no? What about lying to me?"

"I never lied to you," Brock corrected. "I might have withheld the truth, but I never out and out said I worked for your grandfather."

"What's the difference? You let me believe you were just a cowhand. That's a lie any way you look at it."

"I seem to recall you assuming I was just a cowhand the minute you laid eyes on me," he said, bristling at the memory. "You never bothered to ask."

"When I made arrangements with Hank before leaving New York, he told me he'd send his pilot to pick me up. I was logical to assume that his pilot worked for him. And anyway, where do you get off giving me such a hard time about being rich, when you have so much money yourself?"

"I've worked my butt off for every dime I've ever made, sweetheart, and I still work right alongside my men ever though I wouldn't have to lift a finger the rest of my life if I didn't want to. I have nothing against decent, deserving people being wealthy. It's the idle rich I don't have any patience with." He gazed at her pointedly. "People like you, who think because their family has money they should receive some kind of special treatment, that they're better than the rest of the world."

"I never thought that," she proclaimed immediately, but inwardly she winced. Had she really been that way? Perhaps a little, but she'd never bow down and admit it to Brock.

"Oh, no?"

"No!"

"What about your curt little orders at the airport to get all your luggage?"

"That was just common courtesy. You're a man, and—"

"And your threats for me to stay in line or you'd get me fired?"

"Well, you were a bully!"

"And you were a snob!"

"At least," she said, her words firing out like bullets, "I wasn't a liar."

It all came back to that, didn't it? he asked himself. His voice softened a bit. "When I met you at the airport, it didn't surprise me one bit when you took the attitude that you were superior to me. At first it amused me, playing along. I knew what a fool you'd look like when we got here and you found out I could buy and sell Hank's place five times over. But I thought that would happen in a matter of hours, not days."

"You still should've told me," she persisted stubbornly. "After I told you about Jonathon, how could you not have?"

He shrugged. "By that time, it had gone on so long, I was afraid to tell you. Maybe I should have, but that would have spoiled the time we had left together."

Her eyes narrowed into dangerous emerald glints. "What you mean is, maybe I wouldn't have slept with you."

"Think a minute, Jami. If all I wanted was your body, I would have told you I was wealthy. Remember when you told me that you'd vowed never to give yourself to any man who was poor? It would have worked in my favor to tell you the truth then, wouldn't it?"

"No, I think it would have spoiled all your plans to tell me."

"Plans? What plans?"

"Cut the innocent routine. I know exactly why you did everything."

"Really?" he countered smoothly. "Why?"

"You wanted to chase me back to New York. You wanted me off this ranch so you could have it for yourself." She jumped to her feet and stood rigidly in front of him. "Well, I'll tell you something, Brock Jacoby, you obviously over estimated your appeal to me. And you underestimated m determination."

"What do you mean by that?"

"I mean it doesn't matter all that much to me that you intentions were so dishonorable. I won't deny I enjoyed ou last night together, but it meant nothing to me." She coul only hope her pounding heart wasn't loud enough to giv away how untrue that statement was. She took a deep breat in an attempt to steady herself. "You see, your little schem backfired on you. I've decided to take over Hank's ranch You'll never get your hands on it."

Brock casually flicked a piece of fuzz from his jeans whil he struggled to keep the lid on his temper. He'd seen th coming yesterday, but knowing he'd been right didn't mak him feel any better now. "Did you arrive at that conclusio because of me, or in spite of me?" he asked with icy calm

"What difference does it make?" she tossed back car lessly. Suddenly Brock was on his feet and had his hand locked around her upper arms in a steely grip. She didn flinch, and she met his flashing eyes boldly.

"It makes a hell of a difference! If you take over th ranch with only the crazy notion of getting some sort of r venge on me, this place is doomed."

"Why should that matter to you? You'd probably get a better price for it if it went under, although I'd sell it to anyone but you."

Brock tried to curb his frustration. "You just don't get it, do you?"

With a mighty effort, she jerked free of him. With an even bigger effort, she was able to refrain from rubbing her sore arms. "Get what?"

"You don't owe it to me to take over this ranch and ruin it. You owe it to your grandfather to take over this ranch and give it everything you've got to keep it going."

For a long time Jami looked at him, digesting his words. It didn't improve her mood to realize that, once again, he was right. But then, she'd decided to take over the ranch more for herself than because of Brock, anyway.

"Just tell me one thing, Brock."

"What?"

"Am I right or wrong about you?"

"In what way?" he hedged.

"About your motives for lying to me about who you were. Were you or weren't you hoping that the result of it all would be to get me out of Montana?"

Brock sighed. "I may not have told you the truth out there, but I won't lie to you now. That first day, yes. I did hope it would scare you off."

Jami felt her heart sink. Thinking she knew the truth and hearing it were two entirely different things. She suddenly felt very light-headed.

A knock on the door prevented any further conversation. Before either of them could respond, it was opened.

"Here you two are," Hank said, his eyes going curiously from his obviously upset granddaughter to his uneasy neighbor. "Helena's threatening to throw out the whole dinner if you don't get into the kitchen in the next thirty seconds."

"Well, we certainly don't want that to happen," Brock replied with forced cheerfulness. "We'll be right there."

"Good." Hank hesitated a moment before leaving.

As soon as he was gone, Brock grabbed Jami's arm and pulled her along with him. "Hank and Helena don't deserve to have us at each other's throats during dinner. You and I are going to speak pleasantly while we're around them."

"Like hell. I'm no hypocrite."

Brock let out a short, humorless laugh. "Lady, you were born a hypocrite." Before they got to the kitchen, he paused. "You will behave, won't you?" It was not a question, but a firm request.

"I don't take orders from you," she whispered furiously.

"And thank God I'll never have to take them from you," he said grimly. "I'll bet you were looking forward to being my boss, weren't you?"

Brock propelled them into the kitchen before she could open her mouth. As soon as he released her, she took hold of his upper arm and let him usher her to the table. When he stopped in front of her chair, she smiled sweetly at him. "Thanks," she said brightly, and sat down.

He met her smile with one of his own and dropped into the seat next to her.

"Well, it's about time you two made it to the table," Helena chastised them as she set down the plates of food. "Dinner is just about cold."

"Now, Helena, I can still see steam coming out of everything," Brock told her soothingly. "And you know I wouldn't be late for my favorite meal if I could help it. Jami wasn't quite ready, that's all." He winked at Hank. "You know how women are."

"Her grandmother was the same way," Hank grumbled. "Drove me crazy."

Jami's blood was boiling, but she kept her tongue. She picked at her food, trying not to let the nearness of Brock affect her. That proved to be impossible. He looked and smelled too good, and all she could think about was what his strong tanned fingers had felt like when they caressed her body.

"Jami?"

She jumped guiltily and turned to Helena. "I'm sorry, did you say something to me?"

"Yes, dear. I asked you if you were feeling all right. You're hardly eating tonight. Don't you like the meal?"

"It's delicious," she assured her. "We had a big lunch in town, you know, and I guess I'm just not that hungry yet." She was relieved when Helena let it go at that, and the conversation turned to something else. Her relief, however, was short-lived, as the topic changed to the time she and Brock were together in the mountains.

"Did you run across any grizzlies?" Hank asked Brock.

"Not a one," Brock answered. "At least, none that I saw. I imagine maybe one or two saw us."

"Grizzlies?" A shiver ran up Jami's spine. "As in bear?"

"None other," Brock confirmed with a grin. "They're quite plentiful in this state."

"You never told me to watch out for bears."

"Some things," Brock said pointedly, "you were better off not knowing."

She cocked one delicate eyebrow at him. "How many other little surprises do you have for me now that we're safe?"

"Still a couple, I'm sure."

Lucky me, she thought. She kept mostly silent through the rest of the meal, while the others chatted about Brock's ranch, cattle prices and spring rain.

As soon as they were done eating, Hank pushed himself slowly to his feet. "Well, Brock, why don't we have a drop of whisky in my den while we discuss the annual branding and inoculation of this year's calves."

"Sure," Brock replied. "Are you still planning on doing that next week?"

"Yup. You will be able to help again this year, won't you?"

"Wouldn't miss it."

The two men were halfway out of the kitchen before Jami found her voice. "Excuse me," she called loudly from the table.

Hank turned. "What is it?"

"Haven't you forgotten something?"

"Like what?" Hank asked, puzzled.

"Like maybe inviting me along to be included in this discussion."

Hank's face softened, and he smiled affectionately at Jami. "You're right, of course. You should be involved with the everyday workings of this ranch from now on."

She tossed a smug look at Brock as she rose from the table. When they got to the den, Hank poured two glasses of whiskey before thinking to offer her something to drink, but she refused. She wanted to keep her mind clear during the discussion so she wouldn't sound ignorant. She sat down in the chair she'd been in before dinner, Hank sat in the chair next to her, and Brock sat on the couch, facing them.

"We've got a big crop of calves this year," Hank said. "Even with beef prices down, barring any disasters, we should do all right."

Brock took a sip of whiskey. "How many days do you think it will take to brand and inoculate them all?"

"Three or four, if we're lucky. I know it's hard for you to be away from your place that long, but I could really use your help."

"Why don't you hire more of your own men if you're short of help, Hank?" Jami interjected. The idea of her grandfather needing Brock's help irked her.

"I'm only short of hands for this one week every year," Hank explained patiently. "Brock is one of the best damn men with horses and cattle I've ever known, and if he's gracious enough to offer his help, I certainly am not about to turn it down."

It was Brock's turn to look smug, and Jami didn't miss the gloating smirk on his face. "You can count on my help with the calves, too," she told Hank.

"That," Brock said with a wicked grin, "I would pay to see."

Jami struggled to keep her voice level. "I'll bet I can out-ride you, cowboy."

"And can you also outrope me?"

He had her there. "No, but I can cut the calves out as well as you."

Brock chuckled in amusement. "We'll see, princess."

While his granddaughter shot daggers at Brock, Hank intervened. "Actually, Jami used to be quite good on a horse."

"Used to be is right. She's too soft now. She won't last an hour out there with all the dust and sweat and hard work."

"Well, as you said, cowboy," Jami said with gritty determination, "we'll see."

Brock downed the rest of his whiskey in one large gulp. "I really should be going," he announced as he got to his feet. "I'm way behind on my paperwork. But I'll see you both next week, if not before." He paused directly in front of Jami's chair. "I'm really looking forward to this year's roundup. And Jami?"

She had to lay her head on the back of the chair to meet his eyes because he loomed so tall over her. "What?"

"You won't need all that war paint while you're herding calves." He nodded, letting a small smile slip out at her outraged expression. "Good night." Then he thanked his host and was gone.

For several minutes, Jami stared at the doorway Brock had disappeared through. She'd expected him to make a crack about her makeup, had even invited it by using so much tonight, but did he have to do it in front of her grandfather? She'd followed his orders to be civil, and that was the thanks she got? She risked an embarrassed glance at Hank. His face looked serious enough, but she was sure by the tightness around his mouth that he was holding back his laughter.

"You don't know how much it pleases me to see you two kids getting along so well," Hank said after a moment with just a hint of a grin. "I'm going to retire for the night. See you in the morning, Jami."

"Good night." Her and Brock get along well? Hank must have been kidding. His mind was still sharp, despite his weakened physical condition, and she had no doubt that he'd seen right through her attempts to be nice to Brock.

Having nothing else to do, she wandered into the kitchen, where Helena was just finishing the dishes.

"Are you ready for a piece of that chocolate cake you turned down at dinner?" the housekeeper asked.

"With vanilla ice cream?"

"Of course."

"All right." Her appetite was returning now that Brock was out of the house. And the cake must be good, she mused, because Brock had wolfed down two huge pieces after eating three times what she had. After taking one gooey bite, she found out why. "Helena, this is the best cake I've ever eaten. Honestly, you should start your own restaurant. Your talent is wasted here."

"As long as my cooking is being enjoyed by a special man, my talent is far from wasted."

"Special, huh?" Jami teased. "You think my grandfather is special?"

Helena actually blushed. "He's a special man all right, but not in the way you think I mean."

"And what way is that?" Jami asked, the picture of innocence.

"Special, as in the way you feel about Brock."

Jami coughed as she suddenly choked on the bite of cake in her mouth. She had to take a hefty swallow of milk to be able to talk again. "Why in the world would you say anything as absurd as that?"

Helena smiled indulgently. "I wasn't born yesterday. And it hasn't been so many years that my own husband had been dead that I forget how a woman looks at a man when she cares about him."

"You're wrong, Helena. I couldn't care less if I never saw that man again."

"Well, you will see him. And if you stay on here, you're likely to see him a lot. In fact, I wouldn't be at all surprised if you two—"

"Stop it!" Jami exclaimed, cutting her off. "There's nothing between us, and there never will be. We're as different as night and day."

"How did you get along together alone in the mountains?"

"Fine, sometimes, but awful other times."

"He's a good man, Jami," Helena said wisely. "Give him some time to get use to the idea of caring about you. I never thought I'd see the day when Brock Jacoby would be smitten with a woman, because he's always poured all of himself into his ranch and never had time left for anything or anyone else."

"Smitten?" Jami repeated in disbelief. "You think he's smitten with me?"

"I know he is. It's obvious, although he tries to hide it as much as you do."

"I'm not hiding anything," Jami argued. "I detest the man."

"Whatever you say," Helena commented pleasantly. "I'm going to head home. Sleep well, dear."

Sleep well, indeed. Two hours later, Jami would've been happy to sleep poorly. Any sleep at all would have been welcome. But her mind and body had other ideas. Brock smitten with her? Helena's words kept coming back to her, taunting and, if she was honest with herself, exciting her. Her body positively ached for him right now. The feeling was completely alien to her, and she wasn't at all sure she liked it. She didn't trust Brock, probably never could, and she should hate him for deceiving her. So why did she still yearn for him? Why had every one of her million nerve endings been tingling the whole time he was there tonight?

She switched her thoughts from Brock to the coming roundup, which she found herself both looking forward to and dreading. What if Brock was right and she couldn't last in the middle of a hundred bawling calves for even an hour?

She hadn't been on a horse in quite a few years, not since she had visited a friend's private stable in the country. Still, the first time she'd ridden then, she'd taken right to it again, although her muscles had loudly protested the next morning.

Well, she had a few days to go until the roundup, and she would just have to spend a lot of time riding Moondust to get in shape. Riding a horse was like riding a bicycle—once you learned how, you never forgot. She could do it. She'd show Brock she was more durable than he thought.

And while she was at it, maybe she'd show herself, too.

Nine

"God, Griffin," Jami said, "it's so good to be up on Moondust after all this time. You just have no idea."

"Sure I do, missy," Griffin told her with a wide grin. "A few years back I broke my leg and was laid up for a couple of months. It was like going home when I could get on a horse again."

Jami leaned over Moondust's withers and patted the sleek, white neck affectionately. Her insides were all bubbly, and she felt like screaming to the world how happy she was at that moment. She never would've believed she could miss a horse, and riding, so much.

"Which way can I take her without getting lost too easily?" Jami asked, scanning the fence lines that stretched for miles in every direction. She'd once known every acre on this ranch, but except for a vague memory of the general layout of the land, she couldn't remember what was where.

"Head her out straight east," Griffin instructed her. "Just keep following the sun, and that rail fence there. After about a mile, there'll be a gate on your right. If you don't mind a few head of cattle for company, it's a nice riding area inside that pasture."

"Thanks, Griffin." Jami reined Moondust in the direction he'd indicated and squeezed the mare gently with her legs. The horse's response was instantaneous, and Jami was thrilled at how natural it felt, how the rapport seemed to still exist between them.

"Just take it easy," Griffin called after her. "Don't rush things until you get the feel of everything again."

Jami waved her acknowledgment of his words but otherwise didn't respond. After walking a few hundred yards, she urged the mare into an easy trot. The horse still had the same smooth, swinging gait that Jami remembered and loved. She sat comfortably in the worn Western saddle, the morning sun warming her face, while the quiet creaking of the leather sounded like music in her ears. She took a deep breath and let it out slowly, reveling in the unique freedom that could only be attained by riding a horse.

In no time at all, she found the gate. It was fastened high so as to be easily accessible on horseback, and she was able to open, close and relatch it without getting off Moondust. She trotted the mare up a slight incline then stopped her at the top. Spread below them in a valley that was only just beginning to turn green were several hundred black cows and their young calves.

"Just a few head of cattle, huh, Griffin?" she muttered out loud. One of Moondust's ears flicked back to listen, and Jami bent over to scratch under the horse's mane. "Well, old girl, Griffin was right about one thing. This does look like a nice piece of land to ride on." Because the ground was not yet covered with thick grass and bushy weeds, she was able to see the terrain clearly. Any holes or rocks would be easily visible by horse and rider, thus lessening their danger.

Jami pointed Moondust toward the cattle, and once they were on level ground she squeezed the mare into a slow canter. The rocking-chair gait was her favorite, and for a long time Jami sat, enjoying it to the fullest. But soon they reached the cows, and as they started to scatter, she momentarily pulled Moondust in.

"What do you think, old girl?" she asked the horse with a grin. "Want to see if we remember how to herd these beasts?"

Moondust stretched her nose forward, pulling on the bit, and one front hoof pawed impatiently at the dirt.

"I take it that means you're game. Well, if you promise not to get too clever and dump me, we might as well give it a try." She nudged the horse into a controlled canter again, and headed toward a placid-looking cow at the edge of the herd.

The cow eyed them until they were close enough for the mare to take a bite out of its hide. With a quick pop of her tail, the cow took off in a shuffling run toward the herd. Jami reined Moondust around to the inside, cutting off the cow and forcing it to run the other way. After only a few steps, the protesting cow made a sharp turn and darted for the other cows again. Moondust reacted immediately, dropping back on her hindquarters and spinning around to redirect the cow. Jami felt the horse move out from under her, and only by making a desperate, instinctive grab for the saddle horn was she able to stay in the saddle.

"Whoa, lady," she gasped, pulling Moondust in. The horse reluctantly obeyed, and they both watched as the cow, now unimpeded, rejoined the herd.

For several minutes, Jami sat trying to catch her breath, which she was finding difficult to do, because she was laughing with sheer pleasure at the same time.

"I guess your reflexes are a lot better than mine," she said to the horse when she was finally able to talk again. "How about if we give the cows a break for awhile and just ride?"

She turned Moondust away from the herd and walked her until they'd gone quite a distance. Then she trotted the mare up to a shallow, winding creek. She dismounted and let the horse drink. Standing upstream from the horse, Jami cupped her hand in the icy water and drank. As she felt a trickle of water drip down her chin, a strong sense of déjà vu swept over her, and she was all at once back in the wilds with Brock. *"Need a cocktail napkin?"*

She could hear his mocking laughter as if he were standing in front of her. She shook her head slightly to clear it, upset with herself for letting thoughts of Brock spoil her day.

Sighing, she sat down at the edge of the creek. "So what do you think of Brock Jacoby, Moondust? Is he your hero, too? At least you can't talk and lecture me on how wonderful you think he is, like everyone else around here does."

Moondust lowered her dripping nose curiously, drooling creek water all over Jami's face.

"Thanks, lady," Jami muttered, wiping her face dry with the sleeve of her sweatshirt. "Actually, a cold shower isn't such a bad idea." She allowed herself the luxury of ten minutes of reminiscing about the good times she and Brock had shared before a nagging restlessness overtook her and she had to get up. She tightened Moondust's cinch and climbed on the horse's back.

Jami let the horse wander as her mind did likewise. Wasn't it bad enough that thoughts of Brock had kept her awake most of the night for the second time in a row? Couldn't she keep her mind off him for one morning? If only he didn't live on the next ranch, she was sure she could forget him. Well, maybe not sure, but she'd have a lot better chance. Instead, here she was, counting the days until the roundup, when she'd see him again.

Was that really why she'd insisted on helping with the calves?

She cursed under her breath. At first she'd thought she was offering to help so she could take her place in the involvement with the ranch. But was that the true reason? If Brock wasn't going to be around, would she be so willing to risk looking like a green city girl in front of Hank's cowhands? She wanted desperately to show them all she was competent with horses and cattle, but no one more than Brock.

Frowning, Jami kicked Moondust into a canter in an effort to run away from the disturbing thoughts she couldn't deny. She had to keep her feelings for Brock separate from her efforts to take over the ranch. Brock was right about that. If she let herself get obsessed with proving something to him, she was doomed to fail. Her judgment wouldn't be clear, and she'd probably end up alienating all Hank's help in the process, possibly even Griffin.

But it wasn't that easy. She would have given anything to be able to shut off her emotions where Brock was concerned, but she couldn't. It would be easier to survive a thousand stampeding cattle running over her prone body. And that would most likely be the less painful experience of the two, she thought grimly.

She tried to shake off the sudden gloomy mood that had overcome her by galloping Moondust toward the cattle. When they reached the herd, she kicked the horse on and yelled at the cows, waving her free hand. The bawling Angus herd split down the middle, creating a wide path for horse and rider. In seconds Moondust had raced by them all and continued in a powerful dash up the hilly incline that overlooked the valley. When they reached the top, Jami finally pulled the mare to a stop.

"That was stupid," she said guiltily to the horse as she patted the sweet-glistened neck and felt the mare's sides heaving from exertion beneath her legs. "We'll just walk the rest of the way okay?" She waited a few minutes to let the horse catch her breath, then they started slowly to the ranch.

By the time they ambled into the barn, Moondust was dry and perky again. Jami, however, had been unable to regain her earlier happy and carefree attitude. Her emotions must have shown on her face, because Griffin took one long look at her and started firing rapid questions at her.

"You feel all right, missy?" he asked her with raised eyebrows.

"What?" she said absently as she slid off Moondust. She stifled a groan as her legs threatened to collapse when her feet touched the ground. She would be good and sore in the morning, she thought. Then, as she led Moondust to her stall, she amended that thought. She was good and sore right now.

"Are you all right?" Griffin repeated.

"Sure," she said through lips frozen in a smile. She slipped Moondust's bridle off, haltered her and tied the lead rope to the ring outside her box stall. She pulled off the heavy Western saddle, and on rubbery legs that were barely supporting her, stumbled into the tack room with it.

"You don't seem as chipper as you were when you left here," Griffin pursued. "Didn't you have a good ride?"

Jami leaned against the tack-room door for a moment, willing her legs to regain some strength. This time her smile was genuine. "I had a wonderful ride, honestly. Moondust went like a dream, and you were right about her acting like a young filly instead of a mature mare."

"So what's wrong? Besides your sore muscles, that is."

Jami reached down to gently massage her thighs. "Still as sharp as ever, aren't you, Griffin?" She grabbed a curry comb and brush, went to Moondust and started to groom her.

"And you're still as evasive as ever," Griffin returned with a grunt. "Anything you want to talk about?"

Jami's hand passed over Moondust's shoulder. "Do all the men know I might be taking over the ranch eventually?"

Griffin shrugged. "News like that is hard to keep quiet. Most know, I'm sure."

"How do you think they'll react if I help out during the roundup?"

Griffin crossed his arms over his bony chest and squinted thoughtfully at her. "That depends on you, I suppose."

"What do you mean?"

"Well, I imagine it depends on how much helping you do and how much taking charge you do. And how you go about either one."

"I just want to show them that I'm willing to pitch in like everyone else. I want to be involved in the everyday operations of the ranch," she explained. "I don't intend on trying to take charge. I'm not foolish enough to think I could ever pull that off at this point."

"Good. Then you should do all right. Just don't be afraid to laugh at yourself if you make a mistake, because I'm sure all the men will. Laugh with them, and you'll win them over."

Another person telling her she had to laugh at herself. Wasn't that what Brock had preached? She was beginning to think that was the secret of life. She turned Moondust into her stall and latched the door.

She cocked her head in the mare's direction. "Can I ride her during the roundup?" she asked hopefully. She knew she'd be the most comfortable on her favorite horse.

"I don't see any harm in that, as long as you don't overdo it. Her reaction time isn't as quick as it used to be, but since we won't be working with anything that has horns, she should do all right."

Jami breathed a sigh of relief. "Thanks, Griffin."

The old man nodded. "No problem. Why don't you go up to the house and get some lunch and rest a bit? Later this afternoon, if you feel up to it, you can come down and I'll give you a few lectures on cattle and horseflesh."

"Sounds good." Jami grinned. "If I can still walk after lunch."

Griffin patted her on the back. "Just stay out of a hot tub. Too long in warm water will cramp up your muscles worse than they are now."

"Spoilsport," she called over her shoulder as she walked slowly out of the barn. "That's just where I was headed."

Griffin's laughter drifted halfway to the house. If she kept moving, her legs didn't ache quite so much. She chastised herself for riding so long and hard her first day in the saddle. The fact that she deserved this discomfort didn't make her feel any better, though.

She was almost up to the ranch house before her eyes fell upon a black pickup truck parked outside. Her breath stuck in her throat as she realized who that truck must belong to.

What in the world was Brock doing here today? And here she was, dirty and sweaty, in baggy clothes and moving like she was ninety years old. Where could she escape to? she thought in desperation. But the only way she could improve her appearance was by going inside and getting to her room. She would just have to hope she wouldn't run across Brock on the way.

She shut the front door as quietly as possible behind her. She couldn't tiptoe because her calf muscles were too sore, so she had to settle for creeping toward the staircase flat-footed like an Indian stealing across a forest floor. Except forest floors didn't creek. Hank's hardwood floor did.

"Jami?"

She heard Helena's call from the kitchen and cringed. She was still pondering whether to answer when Hank's den door opened. There, filling the doorway, stood Brock.

He was dressed in casual work clothes today, dusty, faded jeans and a brown flannel shirt with the sleeves rolled up. A worn Stetson was pressed solidly over his wavy dark hair, its brim pulled low over his eyes. Why did he have to look so fabulous in his everyday clothes when she looked so awful in hers? Jami wondered self-consciously. Her heart raced into triple time as she watched twin pieces of blue ice roam over her body. Then he tipped his cowboy hat back, revealing more of his eyes, and Jami watched while the ice melted and was replaced by a boyish twinkle.

"Jami," he said, his voice deep and throaty. "Nice to see you."

She relaxed her posture but didn't move. She would stand there forever before she let him see how out of sorts her body was from riding. "What are you doing here?"

"I had some business to go over with your grandfather," he said pleasantly. "Do you have any plans for this afternoon?"

"Plans?" she repeated stupidly. She wished she had something to lean against because Brock had a way of knocking her off balance, and at the moment her balance wasn't all that hot anyway.

"Yes, plans."

"Why?"

"Hank and I were just discussing how you need your own vehicle to drive. He has a couple of trucks, but they're always being used for something or other. Since I have to go to town myself today, I told Hank I'd take you along so you could pick something out at the dealership. So what do you say?"

Jami's mouth opened, but nothing came out. She wanted to indignantly tell him what he could do with his offer, but her heart just wasn't in it to be mad at him. He was too welcome a sight, despite the fact she shouldn't get anywhere near the man. Besides, Helena had come to the kitchen door, and she could see her grandfather standing behind Brock.

"All right," she heard herself saying.

"Great. Helena's generously invited me for lunch. We'll leave as soon as we're done eating."

"Okay. I'll just go freshen up." She gulped, waiting for Brock to go into the kitchen so she could crawl up the stairs unwatched.

But Brock had other ideas. He didn't move, either. "Have you been riding?"

"All morning," she replied cheerfully. She waited some more, but still Brock stood there looking at her with a challenging grin on his face. Only when the situation became unbearably awkward did she speak again. "Well, I guess I'll go upstairs now...." Her voice trailed off, and she gave Brock one more silent plea with her eyes to leave her alone.

"Okay," he said without budging.

She took a deep breath, ignoring the stabs of pain that shot through her legs, and walked to the staircase with as much dignity as possible. She could feel Brock's eyes knowingly follow her the whole way. Her hand reached out and groped the banister. She had no choice but to use it to pull her way up, one step at a time, in a manner that was far from dignified. Damn Brock for insisting on witnessing the whole thing!

"It looks like you overdid it a little."

Jami jumped at the sound of Brock's soft voice coming from close beside her. She turned her head to find him standing next to her on the stairs. She'd been concentrating so hard on the climb that she hadn't heard him come up behind her. Then she felt his strong grip on her elbow, and it was all she could do not to melt against him.

"Maybe a little," she agreed breathlessly. Why deny the obvious? "But it felt so good to be riding again, I lost track of how long I was out there."

"Let me help you," he said huskily.

The next thing she knew, she was being swept up into his arms. "Brock," she protested weakly.

"Hush," he whispered, his nose nudging through her hair until it found her ear. "I don't mind. And if I waited for you to get to the top on your own, it would be too late to go to town."

It felt too good to be held by him to argue. She closed her eyes with a small sigh and rested her head against his iron-hard chest. She smiled as she heard his heartbeat pounding just as irregularly as hers. She felt as if she were floating up the stairs as he carried her effortlessly to the top. All too soon he was lowering her gently to the floor.

"I'll wait here for you to change so I can help you down again."

"Really, there's no need for that." Her face flushed in embarrassment. "I'm sure I can make it on my own."

Brock chuckled, his gaze meeting hers. "Going up was the easy part. Going down is twice as bad, believe me. I'll just wait here."

"Suit yourself," she said, trying to sound casual. With a huge effort, she turned away from his blazing eyes and walked into her bedroom. She closed the door behind her and for a long time leaned against it, trying to get her shattered emotions under control.

A few feet and a closed door away, Brock was doing likewise. He sat on the top stair and rubbed his hands tensely over his face. He shouldn't have come today, that much he'd acknowledged to himself right after he'd caught his first glimpse of Jami. After all, he'd been here just last night, and he'd sworn to himself on the way to his ranch that it would be best for them both if he didn't see her again until next week during the roundup. They needed some time apart to sort through what they were both feeling and to give themselves a chance to adjust to their changed lives.

For Brock's life had changed almost as drastically as Jami's had, although not as noticeably. She had wormed her way into his heart, his every thought, his every feeling. All morning he'd tried to get her out of his head, but after another night of restless dozing and dreaming, he knew he'd go crazy if he didn't see her. He still clung to the fervent hope that if he spent more time around her and got to know her better, he would see her for what she was, and be able to get her out of his system.

So far, he thought derisively, that plan was backfiring. The more he was around Jami, the more he wanted to be around her. And he thought he knew her well already, perhaps better than anyone else. Probably better than she knew herself. And he still cared about her. A lot.

That, of course, was the problem. He'd never felt this way about a woman, and he didn't know what to do about it. Especially since he knew it was madness to care about her. She didn't belong here, and she'd never last in such desolation. This was all new and exciting to her now, but when she tired of life in Montana, she'd take off to New York so fast his head would spin. By the time she left, Hank's ranch would be in a shambles, along with Brock's heart. Even if she stayed, could she ever forgive him for deceiving her? Did she have it in her to commit herself fully to the ranch? To him?

His mind continued to whirl in unanswerable circles until he heard Jami's bedroom door open. He got to his feet and turned. His eyes feasted hungrily on her, from her new jeans and pale green sweater to her freshly made up face and long blond hair still damp from a shower.

"You look lovely," he told her.

"Not too much makeup, I hope?" That was still a sore subject with her, especially after his parting comments the night before. "But then we aren't going on a roundup this afternoon, are we?"

"No, we're not, but I'm still looking forward to it. That is, if you're recovered enough by then to get on a horse."

"Oh, don't worry about that," she tossed at him airily. "I feel much better after a shower." That wasn't quite true, actually wasn't even close to the truth, since, if anything, she felt worse. Griffin had been right about hot water tightening up her muscles. But since she had needed to get clean, she'd had no choice. "I'm sure I'll be fine by then."

"Look at the bright side. If you get dumped off a quick-cutting horse, you can always blame it on sore muscles."

"I'll remember that," she said, glaring at him. When he started to pick her up again, she pushed her hand against his chest and stepped back. "I told you I felt better. I'd prefer just taking your arm down the stairs."

Brock eyed her skeptically and tried to conceal the disappointment he felt from not being able to hold her close again. "Are you sure?"

"Positive. Really, I'm not a cripple."

"Whatever you say."

He offered her his left arm, and with a light grip on that and a viselike grip on the banister, she was able to make it down the stairs without groaning or grimacing once. She felt quite proud of herself for that, and for regaining her composure while in the shower. Her first sight of him had been such a shock that she hadn't had time to work up her defenses against him. But now, she was confident she could. At least for a while. She didn't delude herself into thinking she could keep a barrier up against Brock's charms for a whole afternoon. But she would hold out as long as she could.

After a hastily eaten lunch, they were on their way. With the sun shining on the truck, it soon grew very warm inside the cab, and they had to roll down the windows to stay cool. And with the wind blowing through the open windows it was too noisy to carry on much of a conversation. That worked in Jami's favor, since she was still trying to keep a wall between them.

While the ride to town had taken nearly ninety minutes with Helena driving her old car, Brock made the trip in just over an hour. He pulled into a car and truck dealership at the edge of town and dropped Jami off.

"I'll leave you to pick out what you want," he told her through the open window. "I've got some errands to run, then I'll come back for you. Just remember to get something practical. This is Montana, not New York."

She bristled at his warning. "If you don't trust my judgment, I'm surprised you're going to leave me here alone," she called after him. But her words were lost in the exhaust fumes that surrounded her as Brock pulled out of the lot.

"Tell me you're kidding," Brock said, barely controlling his rage. Jami was standing in front of a fire-engine-red sports car, her arms crossed defiantly across her chest. "You bought this puny car? How could you?"

Jami glanced at Pete, the salesman, who was surreptitiously slipping away lest Brock's wrath fall on him, too. She'd known Brock would be upset about her choice, but she hadn't thought he'd react quite so strongly. Perhaps she had been a bit impulsive in her decision, but the sports car had proven too tempting to pass up.

"Why shouldn't I? I'm entitled to buy whatever I want," she defended herself. "It's my money."

"Yours, or Daddy's?" Brock demanded coldly. "I leave you alone for an hour and what do you do? I can't believe you picked out this car. Don't you have any idea what it will be like to drive in the wintertime? You'll break your idiotic neck trying to go around a curve."

"So I won't drive it in the snow. It's the only vehicle in this whole place that was—"

"What? Worthy of the rich Jamaica McKenzie?" Brock finished for her.

"Look, you have no right talking to me this way!" Jami burst out. "I knew you wouldn't be crazy about this car, but it's none of your business what I drive! If you were going to get so obnoxious about it, you shouldn't have brought me here."

"I wish I hadn't!" He shook his head in disbelief. "How am I going to explain this to Hank?"

"You don't have to explain anything! I'm an adult, capable of making my own decisions. You're not responsible for me, any more than Hank is."

"So the adult thing to do was to pick out the one car that's been sitting on this lot for almost a year because no one else in their right mind would buy it?"

"Look, I love this car, and I won't let you make me feel guilty. You love your stupid truck, don't you?"

"Yes, but—"

"So why shouldn't I drive something I love? I won't have to go anywhere very often anyhow," she pointed out. "And if the roads are bad, I'd rather have someone else drive me anyway, because I've never driven on snow and ice."

"Only you could justify something as impractical as this," he grumbled.

"Besides, it didn't cost that much. Pete gave me a real bargain on it."

"Good old Pete," Brock said sarcastically. "Remind me to thank him. Where did that weasel sneak off to?"

Jami giggled in spite of herself. "I think he might have left town. You make quite an ominous picture when you're mad."

"Furious, you mean," he corrected her, but he felt some of his ire slowly ebbing away. Maybe he was overreacting a bit. Still, he couldn't help feeling a little disappointed at her choice of vehicles. It was just another painful reminder that she couldn't be serious about making an honest effort to live out here. She wouldn't have bought that silly car otherwise. And that was probably at the heart of his anger.

"The car is ready to go," Jami said with a trace of uneasiness. "So I guess I can just drive it to the ranch myself."

"Great," Brock snorted. "I'll follow you home."

"You don't have to do that."

"I want to, okay? I want to watch you drive it. I'll go crazy wondering if you ever made it home in that thing otherwise."

"You don't have to worry. I'll be careful. And I'm sure it drives just fine."

Brock pounced on her words at once. "You mean you didn't even test drive it?"

"Well, of course I did," Jami assured him, crossing her fingers behind her back. "I meant I'm sure it will drive all right that far."

Brock wasn't convinced, but he let it drop. "Well, princess, lead the way. And for God's sake, drive carefully."

"Worried about me, cowboy?" she teased. "How nice."

Brock looked into her upturned, smiling face and felt a deep stirring of longing rip through his body. If only she wasn't so damn beautiful, maybe he'd have a chance.

"Let's get out of here," he growled. He turned abruptly and went to his truck before she had the chance to see just how much he did worry. About her, about them and about himself. So much of his future depended on her, and she still seemed to look at everything as a big game. She was, perhaps unknowingly, toying with his life, and he didn't like it. But at present, he was powerless to do anything about it.

And that's what he hated most of all.

Ten

Men, I'd like you to meet my granddaughter, Jami. She's going to be helping out during the roundup."

A dozen pairs of mostly hostile eyes stared at Jami, and she tried hard not to squirm during their assessment. She moistened her dry lips and turned to offer Hank a brief smile. Her grandfather had insisted on walking down to the corrals to watch them work the calves, probably to lend some authority to her being there, she thought. After seeing all the uneasy looks she was getting, she was more than a little grateful at the moment for his presence.

When the cowhands' curiosity wore off enough for them to ignore her, she began to study them. They were a scruffy-looking bunch, with their exteriors toughened from years of hard work, and only one or two looked younger than she was. Not a particularly good sign, she thought uncomfortably. Most of them were too old to be open-minded to women's lib, and she was sure they wouldn't be all that pleased about working for a woman. She sighed, her eyes continuing their scan of the group until they stopped to rest on Brock.

He was the only one still watching her, but when he caught her gaze he turned away after giving her a curt nod. She hadn't seen him in four long days, so she appreciated how magnificent he looked sitting on his superbly muscled bay quarter horse. The powerful build of the animal would have detracted from a lesser man, but it only enhanced Brock's aura of potent virility. The cowhands were mounted on Hank's smaller, more compactly built Arabians, which made Brock stand out even more.

She glanced at Moondust and suddenly wished she was on a bigger, more massive horse instead of the petite white mare. But then, what difference would that make? she asked herself wryly. It wasn't her horse that didn't fit in, it was her. Never in her life had she felt more out of place.

She stiffened as Griffin approached her. Would he tell her this whole thing was a big mistake, that she should forget about helping?

"Why don't you sit out here and just watch for awhile until you get the feel of things?" he suggested amiably, squinting at her from the ground.

"Thanks, Griffin," she breathed in relief. "That's a good idea."

For half an hour she carefully observed the men as they expertly and efficiently handled the uncooperative calves. First, one calf was driven out of the herd into the main corral, where it was roped and thrown. Two men would sit on the calf to keep it still while another man vaccinated it. A fourth man would tag its ear, then a fifth branded it. The bawling calf was then untied and driven into a different corral with the other calves who'd been vaccinated and branded. There were hundreds of calves that needed to be done, and Jami could understand why it took the men several days to get to them all, even though each calf required less then five minutes of attention.

She was just starting to get restless, waiting for her turn to help, when she heard Griffin calling out for one of the

men to take a break. Then he was yelling her name and motioning for her to take the cowhand's place. Taking a deep
breath, she nudged Moondust forward. Griffin opened the
gate for her while a disgusted cowboy named Charlie grumbled.

"I'll tell you one thing, Griffin," he said angrily, in a
voice loud enough to carry over the noisy cattle to the other
men. "You and Hank have been good to me all these years,
but it'll be a cold day in hell before I ever work for a damn
girl, and an ignorant city slicker at that!"

"Charlie!" Griffin barked. "I don't remember asking for
your opinion, in fact—"

"Griffin, please," Jami interrupted. She was sure her face
had turned bright red, and more than anything she yearned
for a hole in the ground big enough to swallow her up, but
she knew she couldn't let Charlie's outburst go without
saying something. Griffin couldn't always defend her.

She nervously cleared her parched throat and prayed her
words would sound firm and controlled. "Charlie, is it?"
she said to the man, who'd stopped his horse and was glaring resentfully at her.

"Yeah," he grunted.

"I don't know any of you men yet, or how valuable you
are as worker's," she began, at first addressing only Charlie, but when she noticed the other hands were listening, her
gaze swept them all. "The fact that you're here at all means
that Hank and Griffin think you're worth something. If and
when I take over this ranch, I'll rely on their opinions and
want to keep you all on. However, I certainly can't force any
of you to stay. All I want is a fair chance to show you that
I'm capable of running this place, with Griffin's help. I can't
do that unless I learn things from the ground up, so you all
better get used to seeing me around. And if the day comes
when I am ultimately responsible for this ranch, I'd ask for
one month to prove myself. At the end of that month, any
man who wants to leave will have my blessings and two
weeks' severance pay to see him on his way. Right now, I
believe we all have a job to do."

She didn't look at a single person as she kicked Moondust into a trot and took over the position Charlie had reluctantly vacated. She stopped the horse, crossed her arms casually over the saddle horn, willed her heart to cease its crazy pounding and finally risked a peek at the men to gauge their reactions. Charlie's back was to her, so she couldn't tell how he had taken her little speech, but two or three of the other cowhands nodded toward her in what she recognized as approval. The rest appeared to be withholding their judgment. Hank was grinning from ear to ear, and Griffin gave her a wink and a thumbs-up gesture. And, last but not least, her eyes turned to Brock. He was merely shaking his head at her in obvious amusement.

The next two hours passed by in a blur. Griffin had given her the job of driving the calves into the corral after they were treated, which wasn't always an easy task. They usually wanted to rejoin the herd they'd come from, instead of going in the opposite direction. A gate kept the calf from going to the original herd. However, it was still a waste of all the other hands' time if she couldn't get it into the proper corral right away, because there was always a man ready with another calf just waiting for her to clear the main corral.

Thankfully, Moondust knew her job well, and most of the time Jami was only along for the ride while the horse did all the work. Still, after two hours her mind was weary from concentrating so hard, and her body was aching from all the dodging and darting. Her T-shirt was wet with perspiration and filthy from the dust that was stirred up from horses' and calves' hooves. Her throat felt as if she'd swallowed a pound of sand, and her eyes were burning. Her nose still hadn't adjusted to the acrid smell of burning cowhide and animal sweat, which made her feel sick.

From his position as roper, Brock kept close tabs on Jami. He realized she was getting fatigued, but he was afraid to tell her to take a break in front of the men. She would most likely resent him ordering her around, and he knew she wouldn't want anyone to think she couldn't handle it. Yet he could see her balance on the horse wasn't what it had been when she'd started, nor were her reflexes as quick. If he didn't get her out of there soon, she'd most likely fall off her horse. Damn it, why didn't Griffin pay more attention to her? She'd listen to the old foreman a lot sooner than she would him. He'd give her ten more minutes before he stepped in.

When only five minutes had gone by, Brock managed to catch Griffin's eye. He nodded toward Jami, then watched as the old man scrutinized her.

Griffin didn't waste any time. "Jami!" he shouted. "Moondust looks like she's getting tired. Why don't you take a break to cool her? I don't want her overdoing herself. Charlie, you take over for Jami."

Brock breathed a sigh of relief. Jami hadn't been able to argue, since Griffin had told her it was her horse who was tired. He chuckled as he realized that even though Jami hadn't been on the ranch a week, Griffin knew her well, indeed.

As he watched her stiffly dismount outside the corral, Brock's heart went out to her. He had the uncontrollable urge to be near her, to reassure himself she was all right, and he didn't care if any of Hank's men knew it. He called one of the hands over to replace him, tied his horse and followed Jami to the barn.

"How're you doing?" he asked quietly when he'd caught up to her.

She turned in surprise at the sound of his voice. "Just fine," she answered, trying her best to sound cheery. That morning her muscles had finally recovered from her first ride on Moondust, but now her legs felt like jelly, and her lower back was throbbing. She wondered how she'd be able to go into the corral on horseback again that day. Her mind was already working on a way to gracefully get out of it. Moondust wasn't as sweaty as she was, and she had no doubt Griffin was more concerned with her condition than the horse's. Still, she was too bushed to feel anything but gratitude. She unsaddled the mare and led her out.

"Here, let me walk her," Brock offered when they were out of sight of the other men. "You worked really hard out there. You deserve a break."

Jami handed him Moondust's reins without objecting. As Brock slowly led the mare around the barnyard, she went to the water pump. She lifted up the handle and waited for the pressure to bring the cold water out of the short section of hose. No longer caring what she looked like, she held the hose up to her face and the back of her neck, letting the icy water wash away two hours' worth of grime. If she hadn't been wearing a T-shirt that would turn transparent when drenched, she would have turned the hose on her entire body. Pushing that pleasant but impossible idea out of her mind, she instead rinsed out her mouth then drank deeply from the hose.

Her fingers were on the handle of the pump to turn it off when a large, tanned hand covered hers.

"Leave it on," Brock told her. "I'd like a bit of that water myself."

She handed him the hose and watched while he took off his Stetson, bent over at the waist and let the water run over his whole head. Then he followed her example and drank heartily from the hose before turning off the water.

"Moondust is cooled out already?" Jami asked with raised brows.

Brock grinned at her, knowing she'd seen through Griffin. "She cools out fast."

Jami looked beyond him to the small paddock where he'd released Moondust. The horse was refreshing herself by rolling enthusiastically in the dirt.

"I've never been able to understand why a horse finds that pleasant," Jami said, wrinkling up her nose in distaste.

"I imagine it's the only way they can get the itchy sweat off their body."

"But they're not getting it off, they're only plastering it in with dirt."

"Maybe, but they dry off a lot faster that way." He trailed after her as she went to stand beside the paddock fence. "Besides, don't knock it till you try it."

"No, thank you. I'll take her word for it that it feels good. I prefer other ways of finding pleasure."

"Really?" Brock reached out and turned her face toward him, his thumb gently caressing her lips. "How intriguing. I know of a few good ways of finding pleasure myself. Shall we compare notes?"

She trembled under his light touch, her eyes locking with his. It seemed like years since he'd touched her like this, instead of days.

"I think I've already read all your notes," she said breathlessly.

"I don't think so. I think there's a few pages you never got to."

When she saw his mouth lowering over hers, she responded unconsciously by meeting him halfway, her lips hungrily joining with his in a long-awaited reunion. Her arms went around his neck, pulling him closer. As their tongues got reacquainted, Brock pushed her against the corral rails and crushed her body with his. She arched into him, the desire that was blazing through her heightened as she felt Brock's obvious need of her.

"God, I've missed you," Brock ground out throatily. "If we had some privacy right now—"

"Brock!" she burst out in panic, his words clearing the fog that had enshrouded her senses. Her hands flew from his neck to his chest as she tried in vain to shove him away. "Let me go! For heaven's sake, anyone could see us like this."

He thrust his hips against hers one last time and kissed her deeply again. "At the moment, I don't care," he muttered before he groaned and let her go. He stood beside her, close enough so that their shoulders brushed together.

"Well, I do," she told him, closing her eyes. "That's the last thing I need to deal with right now."

"I hate to be the one to break this to you, but I wouldn't be too surprised if all Hank's men and mine already know exactly what went on between us in the mountains."

Her eyes flew open and she turned her head to stare at him aghast. "Why do you say that?"

He shrugged. "Preconceived notions. A man and a woman alone together in the wilderness for days. It's a logical assumption."

"Not to me, it isn't."

"Come on, Jami. We both knew when we left the plane that it was inevitable."

His practical tone rankled her, but she couldn't deny his words. "All right, so maybe they think they know what happened. That's still no reason to give them a hands-on demonstration to prove their assumptions."

"I don't see what the big deal is. They have to find out about us sooner or later."

"Why?"

"We can't hide our relationship from them forever."

She tensed immediately. "What relationship?"

"If you stick around here, we'll have a relationship. You know that as well as I do. Look what just happened between us. We can't control what we feel for each other."

"Try me!" she snapped. His cocksure attitude and casual appraisal of their situation irritated her. The fact that he spoke the truth annoyed her further.

Brock grabbed her upper arms in a steadfast grip. "Don't tempt me, princess. I'd like nothing more right now than to show you how right I am. But trust me, now is not the time."

"Trust!" she said scathingly. "What a joke it is hearing that word come out of your mouth! Why in the world should I trust you?"

"You have no reason not to."

She rolled her eyes. "Oh, please."

"I made a mistake, Jami. How long are you going to keep on making me pay for it?"

"As long as it takes for me to be sure you won't be dishonest with me again."

"Well, I've got news for you, princess." He dropped his hold on her arms and tipped his Stetson away from his eyes. "I don't need this damned ranch! Sure it's a nice piece of property, but I have more than enough of my own land. My house and barns are bigger and more modern than Hank's, so I sure as hell wouldn't live here even if I did own it. The main reason I've expressed such interest in it to Hank is that I know how it's tearing him apart to think that it might end up in the hands of oilmen. I think the world of your grandfather, and I wanted him to find some comfort in the fact that if his irresponsible granddaughter didn't want his ranch, at least its future would be safe with me."

"How noble," she commented. "Yes, it would be a terrible inconvenience for you to own this place, wouldn't it? Sorry, Brock, I don't buy it. You forget that I know you didn't want me around here to begin with. You wanted me out of the picture."

Brock shook his head with frustration. "Only because at the time I didn't think you had what it took to make a serious go of this ranch! I thought you would trifle it away, that it would only be a game to you, a temporary distraction. Don't you see, Hank deserves better than that!"

"So tell me Brock, what do you think now?"

"It's too soon for me to tell. Sometimes I think you'll give it an honest effort, then other times I'm not so sure. I do know one thing, though."

"What's that?"

His gaze softened. "I've never wanted to be with any other woman the way I want to be with you. And I don't mean just making love with you, either. I want to spend time with you. I want to see if we can have the same kind of relationship here that we had in the mountains."

Her legs went weak at his solemn words. She wanted so much to believe him. If only she wasn't so terrified of making a fool of herself with a man again. Jonathon's betrayal had taught her a painful lesson. Wariness was the key to surviving emotionally. Even though she loved Brock, she still couldn't give him that last tiny bit of her heart yet. Besides, she hadn't heard him mention love. What was he really after?

"What do you want from me?" she whispered.

"You could give me a chance. Earlier this morning you asked for a chance with Hank's men. Just give me a chance, you said. Well, now I'm asking for the same thing."

"I don't know, Brock. I'm still trying to find out if I can make it on my own. I've relied on other people all my life. I don't want to do that anymore."

"Being with me doesn't mean you can't be independent, too."

"Maybe. But you complicate everything considerably."

Brock reached out to her and pulled her into his arms. She stiffened momentarily, then relaxed inside his warm embrace. "I could be worse things than a complication. Should I take that as a compliment?"

She shrugged and pulled away. "Take it any way you want."

"You know, you've complicated my life, too. Until you decide to stay in Montana permanently, my world is going to be turned upside down."

"But I've already decided to stay. I told you that."

Brock shook his head. "No. You may think you've decided, but you really haven't. What happens if this place collapses without Hank? Wouldn't you go back to New York?"

"I'll make sure this ranch stays successful." Jami sighed and squeezed her eyes shut to keep back the tears that were threatening to fall. The thought of her grandfather not being around was difficult to consider. "I don't want to disappoint Hank."

"I know you don't. But it isn't fair to him to lead him on, either. If you're not completely sure you're going to give this everything you've got, then you should be honest enough to face that and tell him."

Suspicion edged into her voice. "So you can have the ranch?"

"Jami, I'm not going to get into that again with you," Brock told her with a touch of impatience. "You're going to have to make up your mind about me and the ranch and your future. And for all our sakes, the sooner you do that, the better."

"I'll keep that in mind," she said dryly.

Brock stretched his arms over his head. "Well, princess, I have a bunch of noisy calves to get back to. I think you should relax until at least after lunch. I'm sure the men don't expect you to help out all day."

"They'd probably be happier if I didn't, anyway," she agreed. "But I'll come back after lunch. Are you eating in the house with Hank and me, or out here with the men?"

"Where do you want me to eat?"

"It doesn't matter to me one way or another," she replied in her best nonchalant tone.

As he walked past her, he gave her bottom a playful swat. "I'll eat with you and Hank then, since you don't care. Helena makes a lot better food than the man who cooks for your cowhands."

"Always thinking of your stomach, aren't you, cowboy?" she called after him.

"Always." He waved without turning around. "See you later."

As Brock approached the corrals, he found himself whistling. Well, why not? he thought. He was feeling pretty good at the moment. Maybe the four days he'd stayed away from Jami had done some good. It had been sheer torture for him, but now he was glad he'd done it. They'd communicated pretty well today, even if things were still unsettled between them. But he could be patient. He'd waited thirty-six years to find a woman like Jami, so he could wait awhile for her to sort out her feelings.

As he tightened up the cinch on his quarter horse, he suddenly froze. The full implication of his unconscious thought hit him like a ton of bricks. Hadn't he been trying to keep his feelings in check until she'd decided on her future? Hadn't he told himself that doing anything else would set him up for emotional suicide? What if the spoiled, selfish woman he'd met on the plane emerged again? He didn't care about that Jamaica McKenzie, and if she was the one who stayed in Montana, he was lost just the same as if the Jami he now knew moved back to New York.

Everything was so risky, he conceded to himself. So damn risky. But then what worthwhile thing in life wasn't? Still, to be involved with a woman like Jami didn't seem to be the smartest move he'd ever made in his life. And on top of that, she didn't trust him as far as she could throw him. What kind of relationship could they have without mutual trust? What kind of idiot was he?

But he knew the answer to that question all too well. He was an idiot in way over his head.

Four days later, the roundup was finished. Jami was glad, but the days of strenuous labor had taught her many things about cattle and about the men who worked on the ranch. Most of them had seemed to accept her, and she found that laughing at herself was becoming much easier. She'd made her share of mistakes in the past few days. Griffin had put her in every position except roper. But by not taking herself too seriously when she messed up, the other men didn't seem to hold it against her, either. Brock had always been close by, never encouraging her or offering assistance, but merely watching her.

As she sat down to dinner with Hank and Helena the first night after the roundup was over, she felt good. Her body was growing accustomed to the new physical demands being placed on it, and her mind felt sharp and clear.

She caught Hank smiling indulgently at her as she raised a forkful of pot roast to her mouth. Her eyebrows lifted curiously. "What's the matter with you?"

"I was just wondering why you look so pleased with yourself."

She leaned back in her chair and cocked her head to one side. "I guess it's because I enjoyed the roundup. What's wrong with that?"

"Nothing at all," Hank assured her. "You didn't mind the hard work?"

She considered his question a moment before answering. "No, I really didn't. Amazing, isn't it? I was hot and dirty most of the time, but it was still kind of fun. It pleases me to have made a real contribution."

"So you haven't changed your mind yet about staying on?" he asked carefully.

"No. Have you changed your mind about wanting me to?"

"No. But I can't help wondering what will happen when the newness wears off."

Jami sighed and started to eat again. "Now you sound like Brock."

"The way he cares about you, I'm not surprised to hear he's concerned about your future."

"The way he cares about me?" Jami prompted.

"The man can't keep his eyes off of you, girl. Don't try to tell me you never noticed," Hank scoffed.

"I've noticed."

"So do you think something permanent might come out of your relationship?"

"Like marriage?" she clarified, trying not to choke on the word.

"Yes."

"No."

"Why the hell not?" Hank growled impatiently. "You two are perfect for each other."

Jami suddenly lost her appetite. She got up and carried her plate of half-eaten food to the sink. "Sometimes I think you asked me out here to fix me up with Brock and you're only using the ranch as a cover-up," she muttered.

"That's ridiculous," he protested immediately. "But you can't blame an old man for wanting what's best for his granddaughter, his ranch and his favorite neighbor. If you two got married and combined the two ranches, it would be the ultimate solution for everyone.''

''Not for me, it wouldn't.''

Hank started to speak, but his words were lost in a fitful coughing spell that lasted for over a minute. ''What have you got against him, anyway?'' he finally managed to get out.

''You've been coughing too much lately,'' Jami commented worriedly. ''You should see a doctor.''

''I already have, and don't change the subject. What have you got against Brock?''

''I can't trust him,'' she said simply. ''How could I marry a man I didn't trust?''

''Why, Brock is one of the most honest and trustworthy men I've ever known. How can you say such a thing?''

''I have my reasons.''

''And he must have had his for whatever it is he did to make you not trust him. Give the man a chance.''

''Did Brock ask you to make a pitch for him like this?''

Hank snorted. ''Of course not. I doubt he needs my help, anyway. You'll come around eventually.''

''You're an infuriating matchmaker, you know that?''

''Your grandfather's right, Jami,'' Helena broke in, unable to keep silent any longer. ''It would be perfect if you and Brock got married.''

''Don't you start on me, too,'' Jami said, groaning. ''What would be so awful about me running this ranch without Brock as my husband? Besides, if we did get married, he'd do all the running. He would never think I knew enough for it to be an equal partnership.''

''Jami, you could probably work the rest of your life on this place and never know half as much about ranching and cattle as Brock does,'' Hank said gently.

''Then why don't you just sell him your ranch and be done with it? You'd really rather have him in charge of it anyway. I don't know why you asked me out here,'' she cried out, hurt from his words bringing unwanted tears to her eyes. She lurched out of the kitchen and ran to her room.

Didn't he think she was trying? Didn't he think she was going to do her best to make him proud of her? How could he say such an awful thing to her? She sat heavily in the wooden rocker by the window and started it in motion. The smooth rocking did nothing to soothe her, and in no time she was up again, pacing restlessly around the room.

Everyone was pushing her to get together with Brock. She'd never been one who liked to be pushed. Nine times out of ten, when someone pushed, she pulled back twice as hard. She'd always liked to make her own decisions, run her own life. But she had to admit until she'd come to Montana, the most meaningful decisions she'd made concerned choosing a restaurant to suit her mood at the moment. It was no wonder everyone questioned her judgment, she thought in disgust. She'd had no experience being in charge of anything of importance. Who knew that she wouldn't crack under pressure? She didn't even know herself.

Her self-examination was interrupted by a soft knock on the door followed by Hank calling her name. She quickly brushed a few errant tears off her cheeks and looked around the room in a sudden sense of panic. She didn't want to talk to her grandfather right now.

"Jami?" Hank said again. "Please, let me in. I have to talk to you."

She sat on the edge of the bed and let out a deep sigh. "You've said enough already."

"No, I haven't." The doorknob twisted. "I'm coming in."

Jami watched in silence as he made his way to the bed and sat beside her. Her eyes remained glued to the carpet.

"I'm sorry, Jami. I spoke hastily, but what I said was true. I think you know that, don't you?" he asked softly.

She nodded slowly. "But I still want to try. I have to try," she added urgently. "Myself. You shouldn't have asked me to in the first place unless you really meant it."

"Oh, I meant it. Every last word. There's no one else I'd rather leave this ranch to than you, and that will never change. Even if things don't work out for you here, I'll always be grateful for the time we had together. Seeing you working on my ranch, taking an interest in everything, has meant more to me than you could ever know."

She sniffled. "Really?"

"Really." He patted her knee. "Do you forgive me for what I said?"

"There's nothing to forgive. But if you just give me a..."

Hank twisted his head to the side. "A what?"

A chance, was what she was about to say, but that word was being used too much lately. Everyone seemed to want the chance to prove something to somebody.

"A little time," she said instead. For time was her ally now. Time would give her the opportunity to show Hank, his men, Brock, even herself that she was capable of running the ranch, after time gave her the opportunity to learn how. And maybe in time she could learn to trust Brock, to love him without reservation and to accept him freely.

But as Hank started in with another serious coughing spell that took him out of the room, time was the one thing she hoped she would have enough of.

Eleven

As the next two weeks went by without Hank's health worsening, Jami tried to convince herself she needn't worry so much about him. However, the uneasy feeling that something wasn't right continued to grow inside her. She nagged constantly at him to see a doctor, but he steadfastly refused. Even Helena was closemouthed about Hank's health, and she began to wonder if there was more wrong with her grandfather than anyone would tell her.

She was surprised at how much her grandfather had come to mean to her these past few weeks. She understood him far better now than she had as a child, and she no longer found him difficult to get close to. He could be impatient and cantankerous at times, but he was straightforward and honorable to a fault, unlike any other man she'd known.

Her afternoons were spent with Hank teaching her about the bloodlines of his horses and cattle, which she still struggled with, and his complicated book work, which she picked up fairly quickly. He went over the components of good feed and the nutritional demands of all his animals. She studied maps and plots of his land and the fence lines. He showed her how to analyze the market trends and to predict the best time to sell. At night, she would pore over cattle journals until the printed words would blur and she'd drift off to sleep. Her mornings belonged to Griffin, who showed her all the practical applications of the things she was learning from Hank and from her reading.

She was so busy she had little time to ponder about Brock, which suited her just fine. If something were to happen to prevent her from staying in Montana, it would be better not to see him any more than she had to, so it wouldn't be such a devastating blow when she left.

So, when Brock invited her out to dinner two weeks after the roundup, she was almost reluctant to accept. But the sound of his warm voice over the phone was too much for her, and she heard herself agreeing quickly before she had time to talk herself out of it.

As she dressed carefully for the evening in a slim black skirt and a lacy red blouse, she realized just how much she'd missed being with him. She'd seen him twice briefly since the roundup, and they hadn't had a chance to be alone either time. Had Brock deliberately planned it this way? Had he known how hungry she'd be to see him if he stayed away for awhile?

"Date with Brock?" Hank asked her as she strode down the stairs.

She patted his shoulder as she passed his easy chair in the living room. "How'd you guess?"

"I haven't seen you get dressed up so fancy for anyone else around here," Hank commented dryly. "Where's he taking you?"

"Some restaurant in town. I can't remember the name." She hesitated as she slipped into her high-heeled black pumps. "Do you think I'm dressed all right?"

Hank chuckled. "Jami, you look so classy I wish you'd wear a sign on your back that says you're my granddaughter so everyone would know you were related to me."

"I doubt that's necessary. The way news travels in small towns, I'm sure everyone who sees me will know exactly who I am." She sat nervously on the edge of the couch and smoothed her freshly washed hair. "You're sure I won't stand out at the restaurant?"

"You'd stand out anywhere you went, no matter what you wore. Now stop worrying. You look just fine."

She stood and paced the room. "You're good for my ego, Hank. But if everyone else there is dressed in blue jeans and T-shirts, I'm holding you personally responsible."

"Country folks like to dress up when they go out, too," Hank said reassuringly. "You won't be out of place."

Jami still wasn't convinced, but she'd been more afraid of underdressing than overdressing, so she'd chosen this outfit. She also wanted to look nice for Brock, to remind him of her feminine curves, which weren't flattered as much in the denim he'd seen her in lately.

She heard Brock's truck approaching long before she could see it, and her pulse quickened immediately at the sound of the engine. At his firm knocking, she opened the front door with trembling fingers. He stepped into the entryway, his size and familiar scent filling the small space.

Her eyes danced over the stunning picture he made, clothed in black dress slacks, a white sweater and a black suit coat. When her gaze lifted to his face again, she caught him similarly appraising her. When his eyes finally stopped devouring her, they settled on her flushed face. For a long time they simply stared at one another, until a low whistle from Hank startled them both.

"My, my, I haven't seen a more handsome couple since Maureen and I used to step out for a night on the town," Hank said.

Jami turned to smile gently at him. He seldom spoke of her grandmother, although she knew how much he'd worshiped her. She'd died when Jami was very young, so Jami had no recollection of her, but she'd seen plenty of pictures. "She was a beautiful woman. I'll bet you two looked great together."

"It was a long time ago, of course, but I remember how she looked when she was your age just like it was yesterday. She—" But his words were cut off in a fit of severe coughing.

Jami rushed to his side and took his hand while he fought to catch his breath. "That cough is so horrible! I don't know why you won't give in and go to the doctor," she chastised him.

"I'm fine," he told her with a wave of his hand. "Now go on and get out of here."

"Are you sure you're all right?"

"Yes! Brock, get her out of here, will you?"

Grinning, Brock went to Jami and took her arm. "Whatever you say, Hank. Take care of yourself."

"And you take care of my granddaughter," Hank countered with a wink.

Brock returned the old man's wink with a devilish one of his own. "I have every intention of doing just that."

"Good night," Jami called over her shoulder as Brock pulled her outside. The door was no sooner closed than she found herself wrapped in the circle of his arms.

"You look fabulous," he said huskily.

"You look pretty fabulous yourself, cowboy." Her fingers absently twirled an errant thread on his sweater. "I haven't overdressed have I?"

"Well," he said seriously, "actually you have."

She went rigid in his arms. "What? I have?"

"Yes." His head lowered to nuzzle her neck. "It would have been better if you were in a complete state of undress."

She gave him a playful shove. "You beast. You had me worried for a minute."

"Now if you had asked me if you were dressed appropriately for the restaurant, I would've said yes. It's not my fault you weren't quite clear with your question."

She trembled as his tongue lazily outlined the contours of her ear. She could feel his heart pounding erratically, matching the wild pace of hers.

"Lilacs," he said quietly.

"What?"

"Lilacs. You still smell like lilacs."

She suddenly felt very shaky at the blatant reminder of the night they had laid naked in each other's arms. "I—"

"Hush. I can't wait another second to do this."

Her eyes widened fleetingly before closing as his mouth covered hers. His lips were hot and demanding, and his kiss was deep and provocative. The intensity of desire that erupted in her was shocking, and just as she was trying to control it, he dragged his mouth away.

"Well, now that I have that out of the way, shall we go?"

She didn't miss the unsteadiness in his voice, so despite his glib tone she knew he'd been as affected as she was by their kiss. She didn't trust her voice, so she merely nodded.

As soon as they stepped inside the quaint country restaurant, Jami was relieved about her choice of attire. Almost everyone was dressed up at least as much as she was, although most of the women weren't in colors as flamboyant as her brilliant red blouse. Several people called out greetings to Brock as they were shown to their table, and she was grateful he didn't stop to chat with any of them.

Brock held her chair for her as she sat down, and she smiled teasingly at him. "I said it once before, and I'll say it again. Chivalry is alive and well in Montana."

"Just being a gentleman." He took his seat across the table from her. "Aren't there any in New York?"

"Not many, I'm afraid." She read through the menu, recognizing the standard steak, chicken and seafood entrées. "What do you recommend?" she asked, closing the menu.

"The specialty is prime rib, and I can personally vouch for its excellence."

"Prime rib it is, then." Prime rib had never been one of her favorites, but it didn't really matter what she ate anyway. She wanted to feast on Brock, and food was a poor substitute next to him.

As soon as the waitress left with their order, Brock sat back in his chair and turned his full attention on Jami. "So, what have you been doing since I last saw you?"

"Learning everything there is to know about cattle and horses."

"I hate to tell you this, princess, but no one can ever learn everything there is to know about cattle and horses."

"I know that," she said quietly. "It was simply an expression. I didn't mean for you to take me literally."

The salads arrived then, cutting off Brock's murmured apology.

"How long have you owned your ranch?" Jami asked after a few minutes of silence.

"What brought that question on?"

"I was just wondering. I don't remember hearing about a Jacoby ranch when I visited Hank as a child."

Brock pushed his empty salad bowl out of the way. "My parents bought the ranch about twenty years ago. My father was a lot like Hank. The ranch was his whole life, and I guess he instilled those values in me, since I was his only son. A lot of people think I took over his ranch out of some sense of duty when he died, but that wasn't the case. I loved that ranch every bit as much as he did, and when he was gone, the idea of doing anything else never entered my mind."

"Has it since then?"

"Never," he replied flatly.

"And there's never been some special woman in your life all these years?" she asked with forced casualness.

His eyes burned into hers across the table. "Not until now."

"You've never been lonely?"

"I suppose like any person who lives alone, I've had my share of lonely times. I guess I never thought much about it until a few weeks ago." He reached over and grasped her hand, firmly entwining his fingers with hers. "Now, every room in my house rings of emptiness. I keep imagining what it would be like to have you there with me."

She had to look away from him, so intense was his gaze. "Brock—"

He stood and grabbed her elbow. "Come on."

"Where?"

"I want to dance with you."

She glanced over to the tiny, empty dance floor. "No one else is dancing," she protested.

"I don't care. The band is playing a nice slow song, and I need an excuse to touch you while we talk."

Brock practically pulled her out of the chair. Since people were already starting to stare, she decided to dance with Brock instead of having a confrontation about it.

When they reached the square dance floor, Brock brought Jami's body close against his. He put both his hands on her back, so she had to keep her hands on his shoulders. He ignored the scandalized looks from the older people in the restaurant as he swayed slowly with her across the floor, their hips pressed tightly together, in perfect time with the music.

"Brock, we're dancing too close," Jami objected feebly, but she had no desire to draw away.

"I know and it feels great, doesn't it?" He sighed blissfully and nuzzled her ear. "Do you feel what you do to me, Jami?" He dropped one hand to her lower back and pushed her hips more intimately against him. "It was like this from the very beginning for me. That first day on the plane, even when I didn't like you at all. Then when I got to know you better, got you to loosen up and forget about being rich, it only got worse. I wanted you so much I could hardly think straight. And knowing you felt the same way nearly drove me insane."

"You still had no right to deceive me the way you did." She was amazed her words came out coherently, because her body was in such a state of awareness and excitement she didn't think her mouth could work. She melted against his muscled body and closed her eyes to the stares they were getting. If anyone had had any doubt she and Brock had been lovers while in the mountains, she thought, they sure didn't anymore.

"I know I didn't. But if I had it to do over again, I wouldn't change a thing." He released his hold on her enough to tip her chin up so she had to meet his eyes. "It was special between us out there. By the time we made love, my motives weren't treacherous anymore. I just knew I had to have you, to know what it was like to be inside you, to be a part of you. I didn't know if you'd take off after a month here, or a week, or a day. Don't you see? By then, I couldn't take that chance. I'd rather have the sweet dreams of how it was that one time between us than wonder in agony all my life what it might've been like."

"I wish I could believe you," she whispered fervently. "I really do. I know there's a lot of passion between us. I just can't be sure what your priorities are."

"Right now my number-one priority is to make love to you again." He kissed the tip of her nose as softly as a breezy caress. "Will you come spend the night with me tonight?"

She sighed. "Oh, Brock, I can't."

"Hank's pretty broad-minded. And I could have you home before Helena comes in the morning if that bothers you."

"No, that isn't it. I guess I still need more time. Besides, I'm worried about Hank, and I don't want to leave him alone that long."

"All right, princess. Have it your way for now." He stopped dancing and took her hand. "Let's get to the table. Our food must be ready by now."

But when they returned to their table, it was still empty. Jami giggled as Brock looked at his watch.

"What's so funny?" he asked, one eyebrow raised.

"I was just thinking about how I've walked out of restaurants in New York for keeping me waiting half this long for my meal. But out here, with you, it doesn't even matter."

Brock smiled. "You've come a long way, baby."

"You're probably just joking, but it's true. I have changed a lot in these past few weeks."

"I know you have." There was a small candle burning in the center of their table, and as the light from the flame flickered over Jami's lovely face, he was suddenly reminded of their time together in the mountains when they'd spent their nights next to camp fires. He'd been fascinated watching her face and eyes reflect the flames then, and he still was. That hadn't changed, and he knew it never would.

"Why are you looking at me so strangely?" Jami asked, almost uneasy at the distant but fanciful expression on his face.

He blinked and shook his head to clear the vision of her by the camp fire without her clothes. He picked up the crystal bowl that held the candle. "What does this remind you of?"

"A candle."

He groaned. "Be serious."

"All right." She rested her gaze on the steady flame. "It reminds me of freshly roasted trout, of sparks that start their own fire, of too strong coffee and of how many different sides there are to your personality."

The heat was starting to burn his fingers, so he set the candle down. "Where did that last one come from?"

"It used to amaze me how the same fire could create such different looks on your face. Sometimes it made you look kind and caring, and sometimes it made you look like the devil himself."

"Really?" He leaned over so his head was perched above the candle. "And what do you see now?"

"I see a man who's about to get his eyebrows singed."

He frowned and sat back again. "You're no fun."

Just then the waitress brought their food, and for a long time neither spoke as they ate their meal.

They left the restaurant immediately after they were done eating. Brock took a roundabout, scenic route home, and Jami sat next to him with her head resting against his shoulder. As they drove, the sun was just setting over the horizon, lighting up the sky behind the mountains in swirls of crimson, pink, orange and bright blue. The breath-taking sunset was so overwhelming it pushed all the doubts and worries from her mind, and with the man she loved beside her, she'd never felt more content and serene.

"How come we never saw sunsets like that when we were out there?" she asked Brock, motioning toward the mountains.

"We were usually in the middle of the woods by dusk. The sunset was there, we just couldn't see it because of all the trees around us." He planted a tender kiss on the top of her head. "Jami?"

"Yes?"

"Are you sure I can't talk you into coming home with me tonight?"

"Not this time, cowboy. In fact, I should be getting home now. It's getting late, and I want to check on Hank."

A half hour later, Brock pulled up to the ranch and killed the engine. "Well, here we are," he announced.

"I had a wonderful evening, Brock," she said earnestly, turning to face him in the truck.

He brought his hand up and stroked her long, silky hair from her ear all the way to the ends. "So did I."

She giggled. "I imagine there'll be some tongues wagging tomorrow about the way we were dancing."

"Hmm," he said thoughtfully. "Tongues wagging. What a wonderful idea." He lowered his mouth to hers, and their tongues joined in a long, drugging kiss that left them both gasping.

"That wasn't quite what I meant," she said.

"I know, but I like my version better."

"You're incorrigible." She opened the door and stepped out of the truck. "Thanks again for dinner. Good night."

He watched with undisguised disappointment as she shut the truck door and walked into the house. Someday soon, he vowed, she would never leave him to sleep alone again.

Jami awoke with a start just after midnight with the suffocating feeling that something was wrong. She sat up in bed for several minutes, listening, but all she could hear was the occasional bawling of the cattle. She put on her robe and tiptoed down the hall to Hank's bedroom door. He'd been snoring softly when she'd gotten home, but now she couldn't hear a thing. With trembling fingers, she opened up the door.

He was propped up against two pillows, his breathing raspy and quick. Jami hurried to the bed, and he looked up at her with glazed eyes.

"Jami?" he said, his voice a mere croak.

"Yes, it's me. Are you all right?" she asked worriedly. "You sound terrible."

"I think this time, maybe I'm not so all right."

"I'm calling the rescue squad, whether you like it or not," she informed him firmly. She reached for the phone on his nightstand and made the call without a protest from him. She was assured the ambulance would be there as soon as possible.

"Sit down beside me, Jami. I need to talk to you."

She did as he requested and took his hand in hers. His fingers were like ice. She felt her own blood run cold.

"Your father called today. I forgot to tell you earlier," Hank said.

"Did you talk to him?" Jami asked in amazement.

"No, of course not. He must have called from his office, because he had his secretary ask for you. Must have been afraid I would answer the phone if he called himself," he replied in disgust.

"What did he want?"

"Don't know. I didn't ask." Hank had to stop talking then as a coughing spell overcame him. It was several minute before he could speak again. "Jami, I want you to promise me you won't tell your parents when I die. I don't want your father at my funeral."

She sat there in stunned silence for a moment. "How can you say such a thing? Daddy is your son, for heaven's sake.

He deserves to know. Besides, I don't want to talk about you dying. You're going to live another ten years, at least."

Hank shook his head. "No. Jami, I've got lung cancer and a bad heart. The way I feel right now, if I live another ten minutes I'll be doing good."

Tears sprang into her eyes. "Why didn't you tell me before?"

"I didn't want to worry you. The doctors didn't know just how much time I had, anyway. Now promise me you won't tell your parents when I die," he repeated urgently. "Promise me."

"But why?" she hedged.

"Your father is a ruthless businessman, and he doesn't give a damn about me or this ranch. I want you to have the time to make a go of it without him putting a lot of pressure on you to sell it for the oil. Now promise me."

"I'll promise you if you tell me the rest of why you two won't speak to each other."

"That's for your father to tell you. It's not my place."

"My father isn't here. You tell me."

Hank closed his eyes. "Many years ago I gave your grandmother a diamond and sapphire ring for an anniversary present. It was worth a small fortune, and it meant the world to her. I hadn't been able to afford a real wedding ring for her when we got married, you see, so once we were pretty comfortable I bought her this ring."

"What does that have to do with me?"

Hank's eyes flicked open. She was startled at the bitterness revealed there. "Soon after you were born, your grandmother made up her will. Since we never had a daughter, she left the ring to you."

"But I've never seen any ring like that."

"Ask your father where it is."

Her face paled. "I'm asking you."

"He sold it when he needed money for some business deal."

"He wouldn't!" she argued immediately. "It wasn't even his."

"You're damn right it wasn't!" His emotional outburst brought on another deep cough. "He did it when you were too young to even know it was yours. I've never forgiven him for that, and when he started on me about selling my ranch for the oil, that was the last straw. Now will you promise me you won't let him come to my funeral?"

Jami took a deep breath, her mind in a whirl. "Okay, I promise."

Hank relaxed a little against the pillows. "Thank you Now about Brock."

"What about him?"

"If you do decide you can't make it out here, I want you to sell the ranch to him. He'll take care of it the way i should be taken care of. My will lists him as second benefi ciary after you, but if I know your father, he'll contest it in court if you decided right away to forfeit your claim to the ranch when I die."

"I won't do that," she told him reassuringly. "I'm going to try my best to keep this place as successful as you have."

"That's my girl," Hank whispered. He squeezed her hand with his remaining strength and closed his eyes.

"Hank?" Jami cried out in alarm. He opened his eye again, but they barely focused on her. "I need more time Hank," she said with a touch of desperation. "I don't know enough yet. You can't give up on me and die right now."

"Griffin will help you, and so will Brock," he said weakly. "Trust Brock, Jami. He's a good man, and h thinks the world of you."

"I know, but—"

"Marry him. He'll be good to you, and both ranches wi prosper."

"But I need to find out if I can do this on my own, and need to know he'd love me even if I didn't happen to ow your ranch." She wasn't sure he heard her because h breathing had gotten so much more raspy and labored.

Where was the damn ambulance?

"Jami?" he murmured softly. "Try not to worry. Every-thing will work out. I know you'll do your best. You're a good girl, and I love you. Very much."

His last words were so quiet, she had to bend down to make them out. And then his eyes closed again, his chest stopped straining to rise, and his grip on her hand loos-ened.

"Hank? Hank? *Grandfather*!" She dropped his hand and stared at him with wide, disbelieving eyes before burying her face in the bedspread. The tears she'd been trying to hold back burst out, and painful sobs tore through her entire body.

Then the piercing wail of the rescue-squad siren an-nounced its progress up the driveway.

Twelve

For the first time since she'd come to Montana, Jami wa: alone in the house.

It had been exactly a week since the funeral. She'd had a long talk with Helena that afternoon, and after she'd fi nally gotten the housekeeper to admit she wanted to go liv in Billings to be near her daughter and grandchildren, Jam had done the only thing she could do; she let the woma who'd become her friend go.

She'd thought she would welcome the quiet and the tim to herself, but by eight o'clock that night, Jami was read to climb the walls. Helena had stayed with her twenty-fou hours a day after Hank had died, and with her gone th house seemed big and lonely. The silence she'd thought sh would relish had become her taunting enemy.

With nothing else to occupy it, her mind was filled wit sadness over her grandfather's death and doubts about he ability to take over the ranch. *Who are you trying to kid?* nasty voice inside her kept nagging. *You have absolutely n experience running a cattle ranch, and you think after*

*month you know enough to keep it in the black? Most of
your cowhands will probably walk out, and no one will want
to replace them. You're a fool and you're doomed.*

When a storm started outside, with pelting rain and
booming thunder, Jami started to pace anxiously around the
living room like a caged animal. Twenty minutes later, when
a huge blast of lightning cut off the power and the house
went dark, she knew she had to get out of there. But where
could she go?

She found a candle and barely managed to light it because her hands were shaking so violently. As the tiny flame
lit the immediate space around her, all at once she had her
answer. Fire made her think of only one person.

Sheltering the flame with her hand, she ran to get her
purse. As she dashed to her car, the stinging rain thoroughly drenched her before she realized she'd been too
frantic to remember a coat. But by then it was too late. Once
out of the house, she knew she couldn't go back in there that
night.

It was pitch black outside and raining so hard she could
scarcely see out the windshield even with the wipers on high.
The headlights illuminated still more rain, and it was all she
could do to make out the road. She'd never been to Brock's
ranch before, but she'd studied the route when she'd gone
over the maps of Hank's land. She could only hope, in her
agitated state, she'd find the way.

She was taking the winding mountain roads too fast, she
knew that. Her sports car, so reliable on dry curves, skid-
ded time after time as she pressed through the corners as fast
as she could manage. She drove with the desperate belief
that she would only be safe once she was in Brock's arms.
She cringed with every blinding lightning flash, certain that
each one was close enough to strike the car and kill her before she reached him.

When she finally spotted a mailbox that said Jacoby, she
was ready to collapse with relief. She zipped up the driveway, her heart thumping at the realization that she was near
her goal.

Brock was flabbergasted when he heard a pounding knock on his front door. Who in their right mind would be out in a storm like this? He opened the door to reveal Jami standing there soaked to the skin, with a wild look in her dark green eyes. She stared at him for about three seconds before lurching into his arms. He held her for several minutes as she sobbed and shivered. Whether she was shaking from being wet and cold or because she was upset, he didn't know.

He pushed the front door shut and drew her into the hallway. "Come on in by the fireplace. You're chilled to the bone."

She went with him into the living room, which was lit up with a roaring fire in the stone fireplace at one end and several candles at the other. "You lost your power, too?"

"About an hour ago." He sat on the floor near the heat of the fire with his back resting against the couch, and she sank down next to him. Despite the fact that he was getting almost as wet as she was from the contact, he held her close in his warm embrace until she stopped trembling.

Jami felt some semblance of calm returning to her, but still she snuggled closer to him. "This was the one thing had to have tonight," she murmured. "I was going crazy al alone at Hank's house."

"Alone? I thought Helena was staying with you at night."

"She was, but I let her go today."

Brock stiffened. "You let her go? Just like that?"

"Hardly." She pulled away from him and edged closer to the fire. "She didn't feel right about keeping up the hous without Hank there, and she really wanted to go live nea her daughter in Billings. I knew she wasn't happy her without Hank, but she wouldn't just leave me on her owr So I gave her three months' wages and her freedom to liv her own life."

"You're going to do your own cooking and cleaning? He shook his head. "Unbelievable."

"I came here tonight because I needed you, and all I' getting is insulted," she snapped.

He searched her eyes for a long time before he finally stood. When he spoke, his voice was gentle. "I'll get you my robe. You'll catch cold if you don't get out of your wet clothes."

He was back in minutes carrying a dark blue terry-cloth robe, his own damp jeans and flannel shirt replaced by dry ones.

"Thank you," she said formally as she rose and took the robe from him.

"Need any help?" he quipped hopefully with a rakish grin.

"No. But you could turn around."

"Why? I've seen your body before, highlighted by the same kind of firelight, too."

She shrugged carelessly and didn't reply. Her fingers were trembling again, not from her earlier agitation, but from the way Brock was watching her. His eyes were dark and filled with desire that he didn't try to hide. She slipped off her boots and socks, followed by her sweatshirt and jeans. At the last minute she lost her nerve about taking off everything, and when she pulled the soft robe around her, she was still wearing her bra and panties.

"Enjoy the show?" she asked lightly.

"Very much." He reached out to tighten the belt around her slim waist. "I'm sorry I barked at you earlier. I was just so shocked to see you in the state you were in when I got here that I guess I overreacted and assumed the worst about Helena. What you did for her was very thoughtful, and I'm impressed that you want to take care of the house yourself. Am I forgiven?"

She didn't have enough emotional strength left in her to stay angry at him. "I suppose."

"Good. Now sit down on the couch and tell me what was bothering you so much that you felt you had to risk getting in an accident just to see me."

She sat down by him but not close enough to be in touching range. "The walls were closing in on me at Hank's house—"

"You mean your house?" he interjected.

She sighed. "I guess. It's going to take me a long time to get used to thinking of it that way, though. Anyway, I was feeling quite sorry for myself and very alone, and then when the storm knocked out the lights, I panicked. All I could think of was that I had to get to you."

"I'm flattered."

"You should be. It was all such a nightmare, especially the drive over here. I've never driven in a storm like this before, and I hope I never have to again." Another bolt of lightning hit the ground near the house, rattling the windows and making the floor vibrate. Jami shuddered, but she no longer felt threatened.

"Go on, tell me the rest."

"The rest of what?"

"The rest of what was bothering you. An empty house wouldn't have been enough."

"Why do you say that? I've never lived alone before, you know."

"There's more to it than that. Now, out with it."

She looked away from his probing stare and twisted the belt of the robe in her hands. "Do you honestly think I have a snowball's chance in hell of running Hank's ranch?"

"You mean your ranch?"

"Okay, my ranch," she agreed impatiently. "Do you?"

"Princess, I've seen you do a lot of things that I never would have expected you to be capable of since the first day we met. You've got guts and you've got the best foreman in the state. If you've got the desire to do it, then yes, I think you can."

"You're not just saying that?" she whispered.

"Hey, I'm the bad guy, remember? The one who wants your land. Why should I encourage you if I didn't believe in myself?"

She got up and started to pace in front of the fireplace. "It's just that, in my whole life, I've never really had anything of importance dependent on me. I'm terrified of failing because it'll mean I'll know, no matter how hard I try, can't necessarily succeed. Before, when I never tried anything, I was safe and comfortable in the belief that I could really do whatever I wanted, if I wanted it bad enough. Now I'm going to find out the truth."

"So the burden of what you're attempting is just starting to sink in, now that Hank's gone."

"Yes, I guess it is."

Brock went to her side and pulled her close. "You've been through an awful lot this past month, and you're entitled to feel a little awed by it all. But everything will work out."

Things were working out already, she thought as a sense of tranquility seeped through her. Serenity. That's what she always found in his arms, and that's just what she'd needed tonight. But there was something else she needed even more.

She leisurely unbuttoned his flannel shirt and smoothed her fingers against his burning flesh. She kissed his chest just above the mat of black curly hair. "I want to make love to you," she whispered unsteadily.

His breath caught in his throat. "Now?"

"Now."

"Right here?"

"Well, it's not that I don't like being by a fire, but I was rather hoping we could try a bed this time."

He lifted her easily into his arms. "I won't argue with that idea at all, princess."

They left the candlelit living room and Brock carried her through a long, dark hallway to an immense bedroom, which had one candle burning on the dresser. "See?" she said, waving at the candle. "We have our own miniature fire in here, too. It almost looks like you had it all ready just for me."

Brock set her on her feet next to the bed. "I've been ready for you since the day we got back."

"Mmm," she purred as he placed a soft kiss on her forehead. "Your house looks nice, although I couldn't see much of it in the dark."

"Remind me to show it to you in the morning." Then his face sobered and he took her hands in his. "Jami, are you

sure you want to do this? Just a week ago, you shied completely away from my bed.''

"That was a week ago. It's different now.''

"Why? Just because Hank is gone? Look, it's a natural
reaction to death to want to make love to reassure yourself
that you're still very much alive, and I just want to be sure
you're not doing this for the wrong reasons. I don't want
you to regret it later and hurt our relationship because of it.''

"Brock, I need you tonight. Please, let's not analyze it
any more than that right now. I know what I'm doing.''

His heart was hammering heavily against his ribs as he
picked her up and lowered her onto the bed. His lips trailed
tantalizingly from her cheek to her throat to her ear. "I hope
so, because in a few minutes I'll be too far out of my mind
with wanting you to know what I'm doing.''

She stretched her neck to the side, exposing more of her
skin in his roving lips and tongue. "Promises, promises,''
she murmured.

He untied the belt on her robe and pushed the terry-cloth
fabric out of the way, revealing her already taut breasts.
Supporting himself with one elbow, he traced lazy circles
around the mounds of soft flesh with his other hand. She
quivered beneath his touch, bringing a quick smile to his
face. He loved seeing her like this, so responsive, so warm,
so ready, just for him. He'd never been a selfish lover, but
at the same time he'd never before received such sweet sat-
isfaction from simply arousing his partner. Love—for what
he felt for this woman, he realized at last, could not possibly be construed as anything else—meant giving as well as
taking, and he was more than eager to do his share of both.

His hand worked underneath her back to release the
hooks on her bra. He threw it over his shoulder and brought
his mouth down to her full breasts. He sucked one nipple
into a hardened peak before turning his unhurried attention to the other. One knee moved between her legs, pushing gently and rhythmically against the satin of her panties.

"Brock, please,'' she moaned.

"Please what, sweetheart?''

Her hips arched involuntarily into his knee with desperate yearning. "Please get rid of your clothes."

He slipped off the bed and in seconds was stripped bare. She gazed with loving possessiveness at his magnificent sinewy physique. He pulled her to her feet beside him, the look in his smoky eyes equally appreciative. The robe dropped to the floor, followed by a scrap of satin. He drew back the heavy quilted comforter, and they collapsed together on the cool sheets.

Jami turned her head and caught Brock's mouth with her own. Her lips moved over his with searing insistence until his tongue was ravaging her mouth with incessant strokes that she eagerly accepted. With one softly seeking hand, she reached down to capture his manhood.

A shuddering groan ripped through him. "It's been too long, Jami," he ground out. "You feel so good, I don't know if I can hold back."

"Don't try," she gasped. "I can't, either." His exploring fingers had worked their way down to caress the special place between her thighs. A deep coil of need tightened within her, and the ache to feel him inside her was so intense it was almost painful.

With sudden urgency, he positioned his body over hers. Her legs opened up to him, and with a surging thrust, he had joined with her. They moved together in an all-consuming, steadily increasing tempo, as the pace of their lovemaking grew and grew until it became too strong, too overwhelming for both of them. As the lightning flashed outside, the frenzied storm inside them burst into a dazzling explosion of ecstasy.

Utterly consumed, they lay wrapped intimately together, allowing their bodies to recover while they listened to the rain patter against the window. From the dresser, light from the solitary candle carried to the bed, its steady flame illuminating the joy and splendor of the love revealed in their faces.

* * *

From high atop a rocky ridge overlooking a major chunk of McKenzie acreage, Jami sat thoughtfully on her favorite horse's back. The realization that every inch of land as far as she could see now belonged to her was both humbling and unbelievable. Would she ever come to think of the ranch as her own property, or would it forever seem like it was Hank's? she wondered.

Five weeks had gone by since she'd spent the night with Brock, and while they'd made love on many different occasions after that, she hadn't stayed there the whole night again. It was just too easy to get used to, she thought grudgingly. After all, she had a ranch to run, and for the time being she needed to keep her mind on that.

Overseeing Hank's ranch had at times been quite a struggle, but she was getting on better than she'd thought she would. Charlie, the cowhand who'd resented her so much during the roundup, had quit exactly one month after Hank's death. Thankfully, he'd only gotten one other hand to leave with him, and Griffin had replaced them both with younger, albeit less experienced men. The paperwork was really her biggest challenge, since Griffin continued to take care of the other aspects of the ranch. Brock was always available with sound advice for the asking, and any decisions she had to make were based on his and Griffin's opinions.

Jami urged Moondust down the high ridge as a strong sense of restlessness overcame her. She'd been distressingly uneasy for days now, and she didn't know why. She'd accomplished everything she had set out to do when she'd come to Montana. She was proud of herself, and she was sure she'd grown up ten years in the past couple of months. She felt like a whole person again, and she had developed a reasonable amount of confidence in herself.

And she was miserable.

That was really the problem, she realized. She had everything she thought she wanted—and yet, that longed-for feeling of happiness was mysteriously eluding her. Since

Hank's death, her only moments of true contentment came when she was with Brock. Her thoughts drifted to him at odd times every day, but the nights were the worst. Now that her body knew the pleasures and fulfillment that only he could provide, it kept her strung up tighter than a drum on the nights he wasn't with her.

So what kept her from running to him, from committing herself to him completely? Certainly he'd never brought up marriage or even told her he loved her, but she had the feeling he was holding back, giving her time. Hadn't she asked for as much before? But, damn it, how much time was he going to give her?

Perhaps he was giving her time enough to back out of ranching altogether. Was that why he hadn't professed his undying love for her yet? Was he only biding his time, waiting for the ranch to become his by default? She sighed. After all they'd been through together, she still didn't trust him. The knowledge of that was irritating, but indisputable.

"Oh, Moondust," she said in dismay. "What am I going to do?"

As her gaze wandered to an Angus herd drinking out of a stream, all at once she knew. There was really only one thing she could do. It was time to push the issue.

She'd give Hank's ranch to Brock.

And if her plan backfired? What if he grabbed the ranch and ran, so to speak? This land was a part of her now. Maybe she would never quite feel the same pull from it that Hank and Brock did, but the thought of leaving Brock and returning to the city was distasteful at best, nearly impossible at worst.

She had no choice except to follow her heart. If she had one regret since coming to Montana, it was that Hank had died before she'd had the chance to tell him she loved him. It wasn't an easy thing for her to live with. Despite the fact that she didn't want to make the same mistake with Brock, she couldn't be the one to say the words first.

In her soul, she was sure Brock's feelings for her were sincere. But her brain still needed a little more convincing.

Brock shoved the paperwork on the desk in front of him away in disgust. His ranch was going to go straight down the drain if he didn't shape up. But telling himself to keep his attention on business instead of on Jami and actually doing just that were two entirely different matters. He leaned back in his chair and briefly closed his eyes. He swore that if he'd known falling in love would be like this, then he would have somehow found a way not to do it.

"Sure, man," he grumbled aloud. "You wouldn't have been able to keep that Mack truck from running you over no matter how hard you tried." Still, knowing that was true didn't make him feel any better.

For a patient man, he was running out of patience.

But he couldn't put any pressure on her yet, he told himself. He had to let her get her life straightened out without any interference from him. He had to let her find out just how tough and determined she really was. But in doing that, he was going crazy. He was barely sleeping, hardly eating, and his disposition left a lot to be desired. He didn't know how much longer he could go on like this.

"Hi."

His eyes flew to the door. Jami was hovering nervously just inside the den. He'd never seen a more serious look on her face, and he was instantly on the alert.

"I guess I was concentrating too hard to hear you drive up." He pulled back the curtains to look at the driveway. One of Hank's old pickup trucks was parked in front of his house. "Where's your car?"

"I sold it."

He was stunned. "To who?"

"Good old Pete. It was a nice car, but it was pretty impractical."

"At least that weasel took it back. I'm surprised."

"He wasn't overjoyed about it, but I dropped your name and he agreed almost right away."

Brock laughed. He could just picture the foolish car salesman sweating over that one. "Did you come by today just to tell me?"

"No." She pulled an envelope out of her purse and tossed it onto the desk. "I came over to give you this."

He dragged his gaze from her to the business-size envelope. His fingers were shaking, he realized as he picked it up. A quick glance at the contents was all that was necessary to get the substance of it. He dropped the legal form on his desk as if it had scorched his hands.

"What does this mean?" he asked, his voice sounding unnaturally hoarse and hollow.

She moistened her dry lips, but otherwise showed no sign of her inner turmoil. "I thought it would be obvious. I've forfeited my claim to Hank's ranch. It belongs to you now."

"I can tell that much. What I want to know is, why?"

She took a deep breath and let it out slowly. "I shouldn't be running a ranch that size alone. You know that, and Hank knew it. I'm grateful he gave me the chance to prove something to myself. I know I wasn't in charge of it long enough to be sure how I'd do over the span of a few years, but at least I made it this far."

"So that's it? The game's over and now you're going home?"

No, that's not it! she wanted to scream. *Tell me you love me, tell me you want me to stay!*

"I suppose so," she said dully.

"It took you less than two months to get bored with the ranch." Brock shook his head. "Even I thought you'd last longer than that. Poor Hank must be turning over in his grave."

"I doubt that. He always wanted you to have his ranch, anyway."

Brock threw the papers she'd brought onto the floor. "Look, lady, don't try to ease your conscience, if you have any, by giving me that line of bull. Hank put a lifetime of sweat and hard work in that ranch. If you weren't his first choice to take it over, do you think he would have jeopardized so much by asking you out here?''

"I don't know why he asked me out here!" she burst out. "I only know I can't stay the way things are."

"You miss the city that much?"

She lifted her chin and met his gaze squarely. "I don't miss the city at all."

"Then why the hell are you doing this? Why did you come here today?"

"I told you. To give you the ranch."

"And?"

She stared at him, vaguely wondering why she'd been foolish enough to think everything would work out so easily between them. "And to say goodbye," she whispered.

Brock's hand combed through his black hair in frustration. "Is that what you really want?"

"No, but it's what you want."

"If that's what you think, then you don't know me at all." He sat abruptly in his chair again. His mind was spinning like a top. He was too shaken to think clearly enough to figure out what she was really saying. "When are you leaving?"

"In the morning." She hadn't planned on that, but now that she knew she couldn't stay, it was better if she left as soon as possible. It wouldn't take her long to pack, and since Brock was taking over the ranch, there weren't any loose ends to tie up.

"I'll drive you to the airport." It was a firm order, not a simple request. "What time should I pick you up?"

"That's not necessary—"

"What time?" he repeated sternly.

How should she know? "I'll call you later and let you know. My reservation hasn't been confirmed yet."

"All right."

With some difficulty, Jami swallowed the lump that had formed in her throat. What was there left to say? She didn't know, so she left the room without another word.

* * *

She regretted letting Brock drive her to the Billings airport almost as soon as they were in his truck. He sat in stony silence, only a few feet away from her, but it felt like miles separated them. She really was a glutton for punishment, she thought dismally. It would have been easier not to see him again after their argument yesterday than to suffer through this long ride. She decided the best way to get by was to sleep, and since she hadn't closed her eyes the night before, that wasn't too difficult to do.

The sudden killing of the engine's vibration stirred her awake. She opened her eyes slowly, dreading even now the prospect of getting on the plane and leaving Brock forever. But the sight that lay before her was not the airport. They were stopped in front of Brock's cabin in the mountains.

"What are we doing here?" she asked dazedly.

Brock jumped out and strode purposely to her side of the truck. He opened the passenger door and reached for her arm.

"Come on," he said, his face revealing nothing. "The trip's over."

"But..." The rest of her protest didn't make it past her lips as she was pulled out of the truck and dragged into the cabin. Inside stood Griffin, another man she didn't know and—she blinked twice to be sure—a minister.

She turned to Brock, whose face had finally broke into a grin. "What's going on here?"

"This, princess, is your wedding."

She planted her feet, her eyes wide with shock. "My what!"

"Excuse us for a moment, will you, folks?" Brock said to the other men in the room. He took hold of Jami's elbow and forcibly ushered her into the tiny bedroom. After he'd shut the door behind them, he sat on the edge of the bed.

"Are you going to tell me what this is all about?" Her voice came out traitorously breathless. "You were supposed to be taking me to the airport, remember?"

"And let you walk out of my life forever? You've got to be kidding."

"But what about all the things you said yesterday?"

"You caught me by surprise yesterday. I needed time to think about what you'd done and why. About two in the morning it finally hit me that I couldn't have misjudged you that badly. I also realized maybe I'd waited too long to tell you something very important."

Her pulse quickened. "What?"

"That I love you, hopelessly and wholeheartedly."

"Do you really mean that?" she whispered.

He stood and went to her side. One hand reached to cup her face as he gazed steadily into her fathomless green eyes. "Jami, I'd give you my own ranch to show you just how much I mean it. You're the single most important thing in the world to me, and I know I can make you happy for the rest of your life, if you'll only let me."

She melted into his arms, her body shaking so badly she had to cling to him to hold her up. "Why didn't you tell me before?"

"I was afraid you wouldn't believe me. I thought maybe you'd get some farfetched idea that I only wanted to marry you to get at Hank's ranch. I was trying to give you time to learn to trust me on your own. Your little scene yesterday kind of forced me to rush things, once I figured out your giving me the ranch was really some kind of test." He hesitated a fraction of a second. "It was a test, wasn't it?"

She nodded almost reluctantly. It seemed like a silly thing to do, now. How could she possibly have doubted Brock when all was right in the universe while she was in his arms? She tightened her grip on him. "Oh, Brock, I love you so much it almost hurts."

Joy burst through him in millions of tiny sparkles. "Then you'll marry me?"

"Yes." She lifted her head and left a trail of fevered kisses along his neck. "Yes, yes, yes."

He let out a whoop. "Today?"

"Why not? It seems like you have everything all ready."

"It wasn't easy, either. Have you ever tried to find a minister at two in the morning?"

"No, I can't say I have, but I'm sure glad you did."

Brock buried his face in her silky hair for a moment before releasing her. "I know it's not quite traditional, but I want to give you your wedding present before the wedding." He pulled a crumpled up envelope out of the back pocket of his jeans.

Her eyebrows raised questioningly. "What's this?"

"Open it."

She tore open the flap and saw that the envelope was filled with ripped-up pieces of paper. "Is this what I think it is?"

"If you think it's the title to Hank's ranch that you gave me yesterday, then, yes, it is."

"But—"

"No buts, sweetheart. Hank wanted the ranch to stay in the McKenzie name. Well, I guess technically it'll be in the Jacoby name, but it will be under Jami Jacoby, not Brock Jacoby."

"You don't have to prove anything to me," she told him, and deep down, she knew it was the truth. "I still think you're the right person to run Hank's ranch."

Brock shook his head immediately. "We'll run both ranches together. I have a feeling we'll be a great team." His mouth dropped to cover hers in a tender, searing kiss that was overflowing with devotion and bliss. "Now, I believe we have a wedding to go to."

She molded her body more closely to his, reveling in the tremors that danced up and down every inch of her from the contact. "I hope the ceremony won't take too long, because I can hardly wait to perform my first wifely duty."

"Making me breakfast?" he teased.

"Only if I'm the main course," she countered.

He grinned wickedly. "A woman after my own heart. Princess, I'm going to love spending a lifetime with you."

And he kissed her again to show her just how much he meant it.

*   *   *   *   *

SILHOUETTE® *Desire*™

COMING NEXT MONTH

#559 SUNSHINE—Jo Ann Algermissen
A Florida alligator farm? It was just what ad exec Rob Emery *didn't* need! But sharing the place with Angelica Franklin made life with the large lizards oh, so appealing....

#560 GUILTY SECRETS—Laura Leone
Leah McCargar sensed sexy houseguest Adam Jordan was not *all* he claimed. But before she could prove him guilty of lying, she became guilty... of love.

#561 THE HIDDEN PEARL—Celeste Hamilton
Aunt Eugenia's final match may be her toughest! Can Jonah Pendleton coax shy Maggie O'Grady into leading a life of adventure? The next book in the series *Aunt Eugenia's Treasures*.

#562 LADIES' MAN—Raye Morgan
Sensible Trish Becker knew that Mason Ames was nothing more than a good-looking womanizer! But she still couldn't stop herself from succumbing to his seductive charms.

#563 KING OF THE MOUNTAIN—Joyce Thies
Years ago Gloria Hubbard had learned that rough, tough William McCann was one untamable man. Now he was back in town... and back in her life.

#564 SCANDAL'S CHILD—Ann Major
When May's *Man of the Month* Officer Garret Cagan once again saved scandalous Noelle Martin from trouble, the Louisiana bayou wasn't the only thing steaming them up....

AVAILABLE NOW:

#553 HEAT WAVE
Jennifer Greene

#554 PRIVATE PRACTICE
Leslie Davis Guccione

#555 MATCHMAKER, MATCHMAKER
Donna Carlisle

#556 MONTANA MAN
Jessica Barkley

#557 THE PASSIONATE ACCOUNTANT
Sally Goldenbaum

#558 RULE BREAKER
Barbara Boswell

AVAILABLE NOW—

the books you've been waiting for by one of America's top romance authors!

DIANA PALMER
DUETS

Ten years ago Diana Palmer published her very first romances. Powerful and dramatic, these gripping tales of love are everything you have come to expect from Diana Palmer.

This month some of these titles are available again in **DIANA PALMER DUETS**—a special three-book collection. Each book has two wonderful stories plus an introduction by the author. You won't want to miss them!

Book 1
SWEET ENEMY
LOVE ON TRIAL

Book 2
STORM OVER THE LAKE
TO LOVE AND CHERISH

Book 3
IF WINTER COMES
NOW AND FOREVER

Available now at your favorite retail outlet.

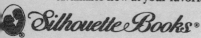

Silhouette Books®

DP-1A

A celebration of motherhood by three of
your favorite authors!

Birds Bees and Babies

JENNIFER GREENE
KAREN KEAST
EMILIE RICHARDS

This May, expect something wonderful from
Silhouette Books — BIRDS, BEES AND BABIES —
a collection of three heartwarming stories bundled
into one very special book.

It's a lullaby of love . . . dedicated to the romance
of motherhood.

Look for BIRDS, BEES AND BABIES in May at
your favorite retail outlet.